THE
SNOWMAN

THE SNOWMAN

Jennifer Henderson

M

ISBN 0 333 21503 6

First published in Great Britain 1977
Reprinted 1979 by
MACMILLAN CHILDREN'S BOOKS
A division of Macmillan Publishers Limited
4 Little Essex Street London WC2R 3LF
and Basingstoke
Associated Companies in Delhi, Dublin,
Hong Kong, Johannesburg, Lagos, Melbourne,
New York, Singapore and Tokyo

Typeset by
PIONEER ASSOCIATES (GRAPHIC) LTD.
Croydon, Surrey
Printed in Great Britain by
LOWE AND BRYDONE PRINTERS LTD.
Thetford, Norfolk

With love to all my children

ONE

The Williamson children were surrounded by an aura of glamour at school; there had been a death in the family. Debbie and Marilyn were also in disgrace; they had not done their homework. Mrs Cowan kept them back at half past three to give account of themselves. They stood in attitudes of abject penitence, being the quickest road to release, while the rest of the school scuffled down the stone staircase outside the classroom.

"We just lost our Gran, Miss."

There was more than a hint of indignation that anyone should expect them to work at such a time of personal sorrow. Mrs Cowan continued to look from one to the other questioningly, seeing neither grief nor any reasonable obstacle to learning a mere ten words.

"We couldn't see," Debbie told her.

"What couldn't you see?"

"Nuffink, hardly. Our Mum had the blinds pulled all day and our Dad kept turning off the light. It was just like a power cut, Miss — honest."

Power cuts brought automatic exemption from homework.

"Besides," said Marilyn, "we was cuttin' sangwidges."

"Sandwiches?"

Mrs Cowan had heard a good many excuses for homework left undone, but never this one.

"Yeah," said Debbie. "You know — two rounds of bread and marge wiv summink tasty in the middle."

Marilyn giggled and hastily turned it into a cough.

Mrs Cowan quelled them both with a glance.

"And may I ask why you were making sandwiches instead of doing your homework?"

"They was for the funeral," Debbie explained. "All our aunties and uncles come and we just 'ad to keep cuttin' and cuttin', and if we stop, our Mum comes in wiv another pot of paste and smack, smack, 'Get on wiv it, you two,' till my hand aches like."

"All right, Debra, that will do," Mrs Cowan interrupted. "We'll say no more about it this time, but you just remember, you two . . . "

She proceeded to say a great deal more on the subject of Marilyn going to the big school in the summer, and Debbie, though a year younger, being in the same class now.

The girls waited, unhearing, for her to finish, staring over her shoulder through the pointed stone windows at the fading light of the London afternoon. When Mrs Cowan's voice stopped they concluded the admonition was over and they had been dismissed.

"Sorry, Miss."

They fled before a rundown on their sins for the last week could begin. Then, grabbing the last two raincoats from the girls' cloakroom, they ran up the steps and across the empty playground to the street door.

"Thought she'd never dry up," said Marilyn. "What was she on about anyway?"

Debbie shrugged her arms into her sleeves and pulled her belt tightly round her. "I dunno. Flippin' nerve. Some people don't 'ave enough to do, stood there chattering all afternoon."

Marilyn pouted. "You'd think she could see we was upset enough as it was, wiv our Gran just 'aving passed away."

Debbie said, "Where d'you think our Kevin's got to then? Wish I were still in his form. Wouldn't mind being kept in by Mr Webster."

"You din't think he'd wait for us, did you?" said Marilyn.

"What, our Kev?" said Debbie. "You must be joking."

"He won't 'arf catch it from our Mum if 'e gone home alone," said Marilyn with relish.

"Course 'e ain't gone home. He'll be at the bomb site."

Debbie was already walking purposefully towards Praed Street. Marilyn turned up her coat collar and followed, pausing to look in a shop window, bright with tinsel and blobs of cotton wool. With slow deliberation she pulled up her socks over plump calves and remarked, "Wouldn't mind one of them skinny-rib jumpers."

Debbie was derisive. "What, on you? Make you look like 'Umpty Dumpty in a egg cosy. C'mon Lyn, it ain't half cold here."

They ran down the broad pavement overlooking the entrance to Paddington Station, round past the posh hotel and on into another quieter road without shops or buses.

"Think it's gonna snow?" said Marilyn.

"Hope so," said Debbie. "Be lovely, snow for Christmas."

The road led to a wider one that had high, grey houses with steps up from the pavement between dessicated pillars. The windows were all broken or boarded up and there were pieces of wood nailed across the front doors, warning would-be trespassers in red paint that the buildings were dangerous. The girls darted down a narrow alley into a mews, and came out by a fenced-off gravel crater that was all that remained of the gardens of the derelict houses.

They peered through a padlocked mesh gate at a limited

9

view of their illicit playground.

"I don't see 'im," said Marilyn. She pointed to a small notice which read, *Guard Dogs Patrolling,* and giggled. "Think he bin ate by them dogs?"

"There ain't no dogs really. You never seen none, 'ave you? That's just to frighten people. He's in there somewhere."

They walked back to the corner house where the boards of the fence met the brickwork. At the bottom was a slight gap, big enough for a cat to squeeze underneath. If one scraped away the loose earth, as Debbie did, the gap widened enough for a child to go through.

"Go on, Lyn," she said. "Quick, 'fore someone comes."

A few minutes later they had dropped below the level of the road and were dusting themselves down out of sight of even the nosiest passer-by. They stayed close to the shored-up gravel wall they had just descended, and close to each other, for the silence and the cold were a little creepy in the semi-darkness.

Then they stopped and listened. Somewhere ahead of them were running footsteps, and then Kevin came tearing past out of the shadows, skidding to a halt on all fours as he caught sight of them.

"Hey, what's going on?" said Marilyn. "Someone see you?"

"Ouch!" said Kevin, clutching a grazed knee and struggling to his feet. "Now look what you done. You din't 'arf scare me, jumping out like that."

"You looks queer," said Debbie. Even in the half-light Kevin's face was pale and pinched. "You getting the flu, Kev? Don't he look queer, Lyn? You OK, Kev?"

"Oh, shut up," said Kevin, "or I'll thump you."

They climbed up the brick foundations of the end house and crawled under the fence. As they replaced the rubble they became aware suddenly of someone watching them from the other side of the road. They turned instinctively to run, then Debbie stopped short.

"It's only our Terry, look! Hi, Terry, what you doing 'ere? Cor!" She had caught sight of a vast and gleaming piece of machinery behind him. "That your bike, Terry?"

Their elder brother crossed slowly towards them.

"What are you kids doing in there?" he asked in his turn. "Can't you read? Look, it says *Keep out* all over the place. What'd our Dad say, eh? Now clear off 'ome 'fore you catches it."

"Oh Terry, give us a ride on your bike first," begged Debbie.

"Go on, 'op it," said Terry.

"OK, we're going," said Debbie, sweetly. "We're tired of playing here anyway. Me and Lyn was just saying we thought we'd see what goes on *inside* the 'ouses for a change — "

She made as if to dart round to the front but Terry grabbed her by the arm.

"You'll kill yourselves one of these days," he warned. "Now just go home, will you?"

Debbie watched him with interest. Since when had Terry been so concerned for their safety? "What *does* go on inside them 'ouses, then?"

"Nothink, I tells you. They're dangerous, like — falling down inside." He let go her arm suddenly and jerked his head towards the motor-bike. "Oh, come on, then. Anything for a quiet life. Only for a minute, mind. And you lot get off home, d'you hear me?"

Debbie was astonished to find blackmail so easy. She climbed onto the pillion, fingering the studs on his leather jacket ecstatically, inhaling smoke, beer and exhaust fumes. Marilyn and Kevin stood speechless and open

11

mouthed on the pavement. She waved, like royalty, from the wrist, at them.

"Ta-ra, you two. Buzz off home now, like good children, and tell Mum I'll be a bit late for tea 'cos I gone for a ride wiv me boyfriend."

The end of the sentence was lost in the revving of Terry's engine as the machine roared away down the road.

It was hard work keeping her seat as she clung to his slippery jacket with frozen, lifeless fingers, the wind forcing tears between her closed eyelids. It was as uncomfortable and perilous as it was cold; it was utterly marvellous. She leaned forward nearer to his ear.

"Terry! Terry, can I be your bird?"

She thought she knew what his answer would be and was ready to counter it, but the words froze on her lips when he replied. However grown-up she became she would still be his sister.

"Oh, Terry! Why don't you never come home no more?"

If he could never be anything but a brother, at least let him be a proper one.

"Come 'ome? You must be joking! What, and have our Mum arsting where I'm going every time I opens the door, and our Dad on about the war and the army every minute, and them littl'uns bawlin' louder than the telly, and our Gran: 'Terry — Terry — that you, Terry dear, just make us a cuppa while yer up' — "

"Well, she won't do that no more. She went last week."

He slowed down. "Went? Went where?"

"Popped off. Yer know — kickin' up the daisies."

He stopped; one foot in the gutter, one still astride the motor-bike. "What, our Gran?"

"Yeah. Mum was ever so upset you never come home."

"Well 'ow was I to know, then? I didn't know she'd gone, did I?"

Debbie shrugged her shoulders, wishing she had not interrupted the ride by telling him.

"What about Cheryl then?" said Terry. "She go home?"

Debbie told him that their sister had not been seen since the summer, but for some reason her absence at Gran's funeral had not been remarked upon.

"How d'you like that then, eh?" said Terry. "Ain't it just like 'em though. Always the same they were — I got the blame for the lot 'cos I were eldest, and Cheryl screams the place down if anyone touch 'er, so she gets away with murder — still does, it seems."

Debbie did not choose to delay him further by telling him that the summer had been one long row over the boys Cheryl went with, and suddenly Terry started up the machine again. "Here, I know. Hold on."

They were off again, screeching round corners and tearing down unknown roads past barking dogs and passers-by who shook their fists and leaped for safety. When they stopped it was by a snack bar. Terry pushed ahead into the steaming warmth and sat down near the counter, where a girl in very short shorts was piling plates and cups with her back to them. Terry leaned towards her.

"Hey, Miss! One coffee and a coke for the lady, and look lively!"

The girl swung round indignantly as Debbie was about to ask Terry whether this was his bird.

"Cheryl! D'you work here then?"

Cheryl seemed less delighted to meet Debbie.

"What you think you're playing at?" she demanded angrily of Terry. "You've no right to bring the kids

13

here — you'll get me the sack. It ain't fair, Terry."

"All right! All right!" Terry put up his hands in mock dismay. "It's only for a moment and she dunno where we are nor nuffink."

Debbie looked from one to the other. Though her family went on if you weren't there, they never seemed pleased to see you if you were. At that moment her eye caught that of the man in the seat opposite. He was oldish and rather stout, not handsome like Terry, and his nose was too big for his face. But there was something about him Debbie liked — something about the quirk of his mouth and the way his very bright blue eyes crinkled at the corners. She realised with a jolt that he had seen her staring at him, and would have been abashed had he not smiled so very kindly at her.

The excitement, the cold and the coke were beginning to catch up on Debbie. She tugged Terry's sleeve urgently.

"I wants to go somewhere. Where is it?"

He pulled away, frowning. "Well I dunno, do I? Arst Cheryl. Cheryl! She wants to go. Where is it?"

Cheryl frowned too and then jerked her head in the direction of a swing door at the back. "Through there down the passage and on the left. And don't go making a noise!" she called out as Debbie got up.

"Who's shoutin' about it, I'd like to know," said Debbie with some heat.

A few minutes later she stuck her head round the swing door. "Cheryl! Cheryl, there's a baby in a pram down that passage."

"I know that, you daft kid; that's why I told you to keep quiet."

"Well, it's crying. Don't get so mad — I didn't wake it; it was crying when I went."

Cheryl glanced hastily round the room and slipped

14

through the door with Debbie in pursuit. The yelling had become more urgent and the pram pitched and rolled like a boat in a rough sea. Cheryl pulled back a blanket and lifted a round, red-faced bundle in a hectic pink shawl. The screaming ceased immediately.

"Ain't it tiny?" said Debbie.

"Tiny? She weighed just on ten pound at birth."

"Cor!" said Debbie, who had no idea whether this made a mini or a maxi baby. "Ain't she lovely, though."

Cheryl smiled suddenly. "D'you think so?"

"I think she's gorgeous," said Debbie stoutly. "What's her name?"

"Karen."

"That's nice. Whose is she?"

There was a pause. Then Cheryl said, "Mine."

"Yours? You her mum?" Debbie looked at her elder sister with new eyes. "Cor, Cheryl, ain't you clever! And lucky!" A sudden thought struck her. "Blimey, I'm her auntie, then!" She gazed rapturously at the struggling morsel. "Ah, come to Auntie Deb, then, Karen, there's a little love!"

Terry didn't stop the engine when he dropped Debbie home.

"Ain't you comin' up?" she asked anxiously.

"No fear."

"Cheerio then. And Terry — thanks ever so much. See yer."

She watched him thunder off down the terrace with a growing sense of apprehension. It was quite dark inside the street door and she crept up the stairs with her eye on the thin line of light round the door of one of the first floor flats. Inevitably, it was slightly open, and the occupant peered out as Debbie passed.

15

"Oh, it's you, is it. Pushing it a bit, ain't you, comin' in this time of night?"

Debbie didn't answer. She felt rather sick as she groped her way up the second flight. There were several Pakistani families on the next floor, and although all the doors were shut a spicy smell of cooking seeped through and hung permanently in a stale cloud outside. On the third floor another door opened as Debbie paused for breath before the final assault. Mrs Purdie bounded out of it, dropping an empty milk bottle when she saw Debbie.

"Blessed Mother of God, is that you, Debra Williamson? Are ye all right, child? Sure, and if ye are, it's not your shoes I'd be in right now, I'm tellin' ye!"

At this, the door opposite opened, revealing Gloria, a girl in Debbie's class at school.

"You won't 'arf catch it, Deb, when you gets upstairs. Your dad's been all over the house arstin' for you. Hey, Mum!" she shouted over her shoulder, "Debbie's back. I seen her."

Debbie put out her tongue at Gloria and went on in silence, but not before she heard Gloria's mother call out in her musical voice, "Come back here, Gloria chile. Don' you go mixin' with that no-good gal from upstairs!"

It was a stiff enough climb with an easy conscience. Debbie arrived with a pounding heart and jellied knees, a mixture of guilt and defiance. Mum was ironing; she did not look round when Debbie came in, but Debbie knew from the back of her neck every line of her expression. Dad got up slowly, gazing at the clock, and turned off the sound on the telly. There was an electric silence: Debbie dared not follow his eyes. Six? Seven? Maybe even eight o'clock? There was no sign of Marilyn or Kevin, let alone the two younger children.

"Oh," said Dad at last. "So it's you, is it? Don't say you've bothered to come 'ome at last, my girl. Sure you're ready to come in off the streets then? I mean, I ain't saying nuffink at all, mind, but are you sure you don't want us to worry about you a bit longer? 'Cos if so, you go on then, and don't mind us, will you?"

Debbie took a deep breath, stuck out her chin and placed her feet firmly apart.

"I only been wiv our Terry. He give me a ride on his bike. And I see Cheryl. She got this job in a caff and great big ear rings and hot pants — yellow hot pants. I think she's smashing." Suddenly Debbie had an over-powering urge to punish her parents for driving Terry and Cheryl away from home. "And," she added trium-phantly, "she got a baby called Karen."

There was a thud as Mum dropped the iron and turned to look at her at last.

"She got what?"

Mum had often been angry, even shocked, but never had her face been this sickly white mask before. Dad, too, stood perfectly still, his mouth slightly open, his eyes staring. Debbie was frightened, well aware suddenly that she was not the only person in the room who knew how to punish.

"She got — she got yellow hot pants," said Debbie in a very small voice. "But it's OK, Mum — they covers her bum, they do, honest."

TWO

The explosion triggered off by Debbie raged all that evening and far into the night. The girls lay in bed and listened to it apprehensively, going on like a thunderstorm on the other side of the wall. They couldn't quite catch the words though the voices were plain enough: Mum's rising to a shrill crescendo of hysteria and then dissolving into a muffled choking while Dad took over with an angry barrage that started Mum off again on a climbing scale of fury.

"You ain't half started summink," Marilyn reproached her. "We'll all be catchin' it for days now."

Debbie didn't answer. There was nothing to say; Marilyn was right. She turned over, pretending not to hear.

"They've woke the littl'uns now," said Marilyn presently, as the wails of Stephen and Carole joined the concert of woe in their parents' bedroom.

"Serve 'em right," said Debbie. She wished she could sleep through it all like Kevin, breathing gently in his corner of the room. Kevin never seemed to worry much, she thought. Then she suddenly remembered his face when they had caught up with him that afternoon. He was certainly worried about something at the bombed site. What could have frightened him so much? She determined to find out over the weekend. Meanwhile there were pleasanter things to think of while she waited for sleep: that fantastic ride on Terry's motor-bike; seeing Cheryl and being an auntie and holding little Karen

18

in her arms. Her last waking thought was of the man in the snack bar with the big nose and the quirky smile, and with that memory she fell asleep.

Things were not much better next morning. Dad had gone off to work early, but Mum's temper had reached the non-speaking stage. She banged the breakfast down without a word, slopping scalding tea with alarming abandon. The school contingent left thankfully for once and arrived before the doors were unlocked.

During the afternoon it began to snow, and by half past three there were definite footprints across the playground. Kevin scraped up a handful of rime and threw it at someone, although it was more of a mud pie than a snowball.

"It's gonna get worse," he told the girls happily. "Mr Webster told us he heard it this morning. A belt of snow's comin' across the country by tomorrow, a whole belt of it, so belt up you two!"

He cackled at his own joke and raced off to slide down the pavement, leaving a long black skid mark behind him.

"Take no notice of him," said Marilyn, as she and Debbie followed sedately. "He dunno what he's talkin' about — it's near enough stopped already."

Debbie felt depressed. You could never believe the forecast and this was probably the last of the snow for the winter. But whatever the weather, it was Saturday next day and the chances of being allowed out of parental sight after yesterday's escapade were nil. She pictured a whole weekend like the evening before, with everyone shut indoors, and understood why Terry didn't come home any more, and Cheryl had gone away. The world seemed suddenly just about as bleak and unlike Christmas as it could do.

They rounded the corner into Praed Street and stopped to look at the hot chestnuts a man was roasting on a little barrow. At least Marilyn and Kevin were looking at the chestnuts: Debbie stood staring incredulously at the man himself. He had a big nose and very bright blue eyes that crinkled at the corners when he smiled at her . . . .

The other two had raced on; there was no question of risking being late home today. Debbie ran after them, catching hold of Marilyn.

"Hey, Lyn — I seen that man yesterday, in the caff where Cheryl works. He sat near Terry and I, having his tea."

"So what?" said Marilyn. "Has to have his tea some-wheres, don't 'e?"

Debbie didn't argue. They were nearly home now and the sky ahead was a dark slate grey coming up over the high rise blocks to the north. Kevin pointed to it.

"Cor, look at that! I tol' you it was coming, din't I, and now here it comes, see, belting up over London."

"I'll belt you in a minute," said Marilyn, and Debbie laughed aloud, for the snow hadn't let them down after all. With no more school for two days, suddenly she felt sure they would all get out to play in it somehow.

Mum had improved enough on their return to say hello, even though she didn't look at Debbie. The kitchen was a fog of frying chips, and this was a good sign too — Mum never cooked at the height of a temper. Dad wasn't home yet so Stephen and Carole were watching the children's programmes. Kevin nicked one of Stephen's chips, but Stephen's protests were drowned by someone ringing the street doorbell.

Mum said something and turned down the gas, and they all peered out of the window.

20

"Who is it?" called Mum.

A female face looked up at them. "Oh, is that you, Mrs Williamson? Are you busy for a moment?"

"We ain't voting at all this time, we're fed up with the lot of 'em," Mum was beginning, when Debbie said, "It's that Mrs Mayhew come about the country holidays."

Most children in the neighbourhood whose parents could not afford a family holiday were sent off for a fortnight in the summer, somewhere out of London.

"Oh," said Mum. "Early, ain't she?" She shouted down, "Push the door and come up, then, it's broke like everythink else here."

After a long wait Mrs Mayhew arrived, dabbing at the dewdrop on the end of her nose which instantly reappeared, to the children's delight and fascination. As soon as she could speak she apologised for calling before Christmas, explaining that she was going on a cruise in the New Year, and wanted to get the children's holidays fixed up before she went.

"Sit down," said Mum, pushing Kevin off Dad's chair and dealing him a swift backhander for being on it. "I'll get you a cuppa."

"Oh please don't bother," said Mrs Mayhew, dropping a bundle of forms and groping in her handbag for a biro.

"I'm making one anyway," said Mum.

"Oh thank you. Very weak, please, and no sugar," said Mrs Mayhew.

"That's OK, we got plenty," said Mum. She retreated to the kitchen muttering, "Just 'cos we don't go on no cruises don't mean to say we can't have a decent cuppa tea."

Debbie's heart sank. This was going to put Mum right back in her blackest mood, just when she was showing progress.

21

"And where," said Mrs Mayhew to the three older ones, "would you like to go next summer? The seaside again?"

They looked at each other and shook their heads on principle. Enthusiasm was dodgy: you could have advantage taken of you.

Mrs Mayhew looked surprised. "Didn't you enjoy it last year?"

"We wasn't partic'lar," said Marilyn, coolly.

"We didn't mind it," said Debbie, who had loved every moment.

"I don't want to go," said Kevin, unexpectedly.

"Why not?" they all asked.

"I dunno," said Kevin.

Mrs Mayhew leaned forward, her necklaces jingling. "Tell me what you didn't like, dear," she said.

"There's dead birds at the seaside," said Kevin.

"You're silly," said Marilyn.

"Dead what?" said Mrs Mayhew.

"Birds," said Kevin. "I seen a dead chicken and I din't like it, see."

"But my dear, there are dead chickens in London."

Kevin shrugged his shoulders. "Well, I ain't going," he said.

Debbie knew this was just an excuse but defended to the last his British right not to have enjoyed his holiday.

"It upset 'im," she said. "Din't it, Kev? He seen a dead cat and dead flies and dead flowers, but never a dead bird, see, and it upset 'im. That right, Kev? Tell the lady."

"And I seen a dead spider and a dead wasp — " Kevin was warming to his argument — "And a dead person!" he finished triumphantly.

"Course you ain't," said Debbie. This was carrying dislike of the seaside too far.

Mum came in again and Mrs Mayhew changed the subject swiftly and disastrously. "How is your mother, Mrs Williamson?"

Mum's eyes turned pink and she swallowed. "Passed on last week, thank you," she said with dignity.

Mrs Mayhew spilt her tea over the forms and said she was so sorry, over and over again. Then she hunted for the biro again and started filling in the particulars for the holidays. Debbie was watching Kevin. He had that odd look again. And it couldn't have been Gran he saw because Mum had locked her door by the time they had come back from school.

Mrs Mayhew rose to her feet. "I don't need to collect any money till I come back," she said.

Mum's mouth grew tight at the corners. "And I ain't got none to give you," she said. "Can't give you what I ain't got, can I? Money! It's all money these days. People seem to think yer a walkin' bank."

Debbie groaned inwardly. Mrs Mayhew said goodbye to the children and then turned back at the door.

"You don't happen to know when I should be likely to catch Mrs Purdie downstairs at home, do you?"

Mum took a deep breath and said through barely open lips: "I really couldn't say. I don't go pokin' me nose — like some."

She turned sharply and trod on Carole's toe, who promptly burst into tears.

"Will you kids get back to your tea and stop getting under me feet?" Mum shouted. "I'm sick and tired of you all crowding round all the time. I can't move for you!"

She slammed the door on Mrs Mayhew, and on any hopes Debbie had left of seeing the outside world that weekend.

Dad was home and tea cleared away by the time the next visitor rang the bell. The top door this time: someone who knew the way. Dad looked at Mum questioningly.

"I told you," said Mum. "That'll be that Mrs Mayhew back again, wanting her money all right now she knows you're back. Friday, see. She knows you'll 'ave it; what'd I tell you?"

Marilyn was sent to investigate.

"Tell her she can whistle for it," Mum called after her. She looked at Dad. "Put yer teeth in, Les."

"Why should I?" said Dad. "I've had me tea, ain't I? I'm not puttin' in me teeth for the likes of her. She don't need to come if she don't like it."

Marilyn came back whispering, "There's someone there."

"Well we know that," said Dad. "Who is it?"

"She say her name's Auntie Lil."

"Oh my good gawd!" said Dad.

"That's all I need tonight," said Mum.

THREE

It was not difficult to see that Auntie Lil was Mum's sister, even though she was half the girth and scraggy as a gypsy's mongrel. She nodded to Dad as she came through the door, and said to Mum, "Got yer letter all right. When are they planting her then, eh?"

Mum's mouth tightened at the corners. "The funeral was last Saturday. You've missed it."

"Cor, what a shame," said Auntie Lil. "I come as quick as I could, too. You sent it to Wandsworth, didn't you? Well, I ain't been there for two year or more. Got a room in Clacton now, ain't I? They sent it on but I only just got it, see. Come as soon as I heard."

Mum looked at her knowingly. "Yeah," she said at last, in a voice reserved for disbelieving people.

"Brought some flowers, too," said Auntie Lil, suddenly producing a weary bunch of forced daffodils. "Wouldn't have got 'em if I'd known. Dear, they was. No use taking 'em back, though. They won't give you nothink once you've paid. You have 'em, Doris. Expect you got a vase of some sort, eh?"

Mum said, "There's a jug in the kitchen," and she murmured to Dad, "Take 'em back! Hear that? They come off of a barrow — if she didn't nick 'em in the first place."

Auntie Lil called from the kitchen, "I'm putting the kettle on while I'm in 'ere."

Mum rolled her eyes heavenwards. "We've 'ad tea," she called back.

"Yeah, well I ain't," said Auntie Lil. "Besides, you can always drink another cuppa, that's what I say."

Presently she returned with several cups and saucers and half a packet of biscuits. "All I could see," she said. "Still, I'll soon find me way round again." She handed a cup to Marilyn. "One for you, dear? Cheryl, ain't it?"

They put her right.

"Cor, ain't you grown," said Auntie Lil. "Where's Cheryl then?"

"She — " began Debbie.

"You dare!" said Mum, with a withering look.

"Oh dear," said Auntie Lil. "Cheryl brought trouble 'ome then? Fancy her being that age already."

"Who said anythink about trouble?" said Dad. "Cheryl decided to leave 'ome and that's all there is to it."

"Oh. I see."

Auntie Lil's sharp little eyes scanned the room and its occupants for a minute or two, while she sipped her tea and munched in silence. Then she said, "Well, I'm for me bed."

"Where's that then?" Dad challenged her. "You got a long way to go, ain't you?"

Auntie Lil looked at Mum. "There's her room, now she gone, ain't there?"

Mum shut her mouth as tight as a mousetrap and looked at Dad. Dad shook his head slowly. "We needs that room now, Lil. Kids are growing up, see. Kevin and Stephen's going in that room. Our Kevin can't share with the girls no longer."

There was a loud outcry from Kevin at this suggestion. "Hey, who says? I ain't goin' in with no littl'uns! I sleeps with Lyn and Deb and I ain't movin' for no one! I just ain't gonna, see?"

Dad said, "You'll go where you're sent, mate, and

26

make no mistake."

But possession is nine tenths of the law, and Auntie Lil was already in Gran's room, turning down the cover on the big bed and kicking off her shoes beneath it.

"Well, I don't see no kids in 'ere tonight," she said.

"Cor blimey," said Dad, "your sister!" And he called Auntie Lil something Debbie didn't quite catch. But blood is thicker than water and put like that Mum rushed to her defence. "No she ain't!" she chipped in. "Our Lil's a lot of things, I know, but that she ain't."

"Only 'cos she never 'ad the chance," said Dad.

"One night then, Lil," said Mum. "Then tomorrow — out. We ain't got the room, see, so it's no use saying we 'ave."

The children stood in the doorway and watched, fascinated, while Auntie Lil took off her dress and rolled down woollen stockings beneath a floral winceyette petticoat. Then she untied a string at her waist and the hem dropped to her ankles.

"Are you really gonna sleep in 'ere?" said Kevin.

"Sleep?" echoed Auntie Lil, unzipping a little bag and holding up a bottle of white pills. "Don't you worry, me darlin' — Auntie's gonna take her tablets. Two or three of these and she'll be out cold till morning."

"And you won't go 'ome tomorrow, will you?"

"Ain't got no 'ome to go to, 'ave I? Give up me room to come here, see. Don't worry, dearie, takes more'n your mum to shift me. Always has."

Kevin advanced a little into the room at this reassuring news. "I love you, Auntie Lil," he told her. "Even if you are a — "

"Kevin!" roared Mum from the kitchen, and Debbie missed it again.

*

27

It was strangely quiet when the children woke next morning, and the room seemed unnaturally light even for a Saturday. Debbie knelt up in bed and pushed the grey net curtain to one side.

"Crumbs!" she said. "Hey, Lyn, come and look at this!"

The others were over in a flash, wiping the mist off the window with hands still warm from sleep.

"Blimey, *look*!" said Kevin. "Told you, din't I?"

"Road's quite covered," said Debbie. "You can't even see where the pavement goes."

"Don't it make the houses look black?" said Marilyn.

"There ain't been no cars," said Kevin. "Not a mark, look. Too deep, I bet. Cor — look how deep it is outside the window!" He put his hand flat against the glass and the snow came nearly as high as his finger tips. He made a sweeping gesture along the windowsill and added, "I wouldn't half like to put some down your necks."

Auntie Lil did not appear until breakfast was long past. She came, heavy-eyed, into the kitchen in her winceyette nightie, yawning and scratching. Mum was peeling potatoes and Dad was searching for his cigarettes.

"Bitter, ain't it," said Auntie Lil, putting on the kettle. "Fright of me life when I looked out. 'Ere —" She tossed a cigarette to Dad and stuck one in her own mouth. "Have one of mine. Fair's fair; I'm drinking your tea."

Dad hesitated: it was difficult to accept her fags and give her notice to quit in the same breath, but desperation soon drove him to succeeding. Auntie Lil appealed to the children.

"Nasty, your dad. Mean streak, ain't he. Can't 'ave looked out this morning. Blimey — only fit for eskimoes, and I ain't got only the one pair of shoes I come in. You

28

wouldn't turn poor old Auntie out in the cold, would you?"

Kevin said, "I don't want you to go."

Debbie and Marilyn, although with less axe to grind, supported him.

Mum spun round from the sink brandishing the potato peeler. "That's enough from you kids! You don't know nothink about it. Here, you three, just get out of my hair for a bit! Outside, I say, I don't care if it is cold — I'm not 'aving you lot under me feet all day. Out, all of you, and don't come back till dinner."

They were gone past recall before she could change her mind.

It was like stepping ashore in a foreign country: the street, the familiar landmarks, even the freezing air were different. Gingerly, they trod into white banks that crunched softly underfoot, like biting into home-made fudge. Then Kevin swept an avalanche of snow off the roof of a parked car onto his sisters, and after that they were running, shrieking and floundering in unspoken agreement towards the inevitable destination.

The bombed site lay untouched, like a sheet of paper before the drawing lesson. For a while they bombarded each other, and then, joined by other children, they split into groups: Kevin to continue snowball warfare with the boys, and his sisters to make a snowman with Bernadette Purdie and Gloria. The snow was perfect: just sticky enough to roll up in great fluffy bales like cotton wool. They made two huge ones for the body and then a smaller one for the head, moulding extra hand-fuls onto the sides for arms. Marilyn pushed stones down the middle of the top half for buttons and Gloria added padding to the shoulders, the backs of her hands incongruously dark against the snow.

Debbie jumped up and down with pleasure on numbed feet, her breath steaming like a boiling kettle.

"Oh, he's lovely! He's lovely! C'mon, let's give him eyes and teeth!"

She found two round stones, and then some small ones to place curving upwards in a wide smile, while a snowball stuck in the middle of it all served for his nose. Then she stood back, gazing at the snowman in amazement. There was no doubt about it; she recognised him, she knew him! He was the dead spit of the Praed Street chestnut seller who had his tea in Cheryl's cafe. She looked round to point this out to Marilyn and saw Kevin coming towards them, blowing on his hands, his teeth chattering.

"Let's pack it in," he said. "I'm froze."

Most of the children were soaked through by this time, and were drifting away in twos and threes. The Williamsons followed suit a little way behind the others. When they reached the usual exit they stopped short and listened. There were voices the other side of the fence: stern, authoritative voices and meek, childish ones. Kevin peered through a knot hole and ducked quickly.

"Blimey," he whispered. "It's the fuzz. Two of 'em, and they caught someone."

They heard names and addresses being handed over, and then:

"Are there any more of you in there?"

"I dunno. Yeah, two or three, maybe."

There was a final warning, then running footsteps as the miscreants were released. Presently, after further grown-up murmurs, there was silence. Kevin had another look and signalled to the girls to move further from the fence.

"One's gone," he whispered, "but one's just stood there like a flipping cat sat over a mouse 'ole. What we gonna do?"

There was a pause, then Debbie said, "They let them others go. They can't eat you."

Kevin said, "They took it all down, though, din't they. Can't you just see our Dad when they comes round tonight and tells him? Ain't you been in enough trouble lately?"

Debbie had.

"I wants me dinner," said Marilyn. "And I'm 'arf froze, stood 'ere."

"Oh, come on," said Debbie. "We'll get through them houses somehow."

Kevin grabbed at her raincoat. "No don't! They ain't safe — you heard our Terry say so."

But Debbie was off, running along the backs of the houses, looking for the weak spot she knew Kevin had already found. It wasn't difficult; he himself gave the game away by giving a wide berth to a french window that had been boarded up. She stopped, turning back to investigate, and an icy wind shivered one of the boards where the nails had come out at the bottom. She pushed it sideways and its neighbour gave a bit too, making a narrow opening, black in the glare of the snow.

"Go on, get in, you two, before they sees us."

Debbie was the only one who got through easily. Marilyn got stuck and grazed her shins in her anxiety to reach safety. Kevin, although the smallest, had to be forced through.

They looked round the derelict room in which they found themselves. It was dim, bare and cold, but Debbie could see nothing to terrify.

"Well," she said sharply to Kevin, "what are you

31

snivelling about then? Better'n being caught, ain't it?"

Kevin wiped his nose on his sleeve and said nothing. They looked cautiously out of a window that still contained some jagged panes of glass, but saw no one. The bombed site looked inexpressibly dreary now that all the children had gone. The snowman stood out bleak and lonely against a surface scribbled all over with dark furrows.

"How long've we gotta stay here for?" said Marilyn, dancing up and down. "Me feet are falling off."

"Better give it a little," Debbie counselled. "Keep still, can't you? You're making the whole floor bounce — we'll go through in a minute!"

They stood listening by the window, watching for the dark uniformed figure at the mesh gate at the other end, but no one appeared.

"Sh!" said Debbie suddenly. "Thought I heard summink."

They all turned round quickly. There, in the far corner, where there had certainly not been anyone before, was a man sitting on the floor, his hands clasping his knees, quietly smiling at them.

"I seen you," said Debbie at last. "In Cheryl's caff."

He bowed slightly. "The pleasure was mine," he said.

"You're the bloke what sells chestnuts, ain't you?" said Kevin.

"I have that honour," said the man.

"You looks just like our snowman to me," said Marilyn.

"I am flattered, my dear."

Debbie said to Kevin, "Was it him you saw here before, what scared you?"

Kevin shook his head. "The one I saw was younger." Then he added, "And dead."

32

She turned to the stranger.

"Then who are you?"

The bright blue eyes looked very much alive.

"I am an angel."

"A *angel*?"

They looked at him with varying expressions of disbelief.

"Go on," said Kevin. "Yer too fat."

"Pull the other one," said Marilyn, "it's got bells on."

Debbie eyed him shrewdly. "Where's yer feathers then, eh?"

"My dear child," said the stranger, "this is the twentieth century. If I were to walk up and down Edgware Road with six-foot wings sprouting from my shoulders, what in the world do you think people would say?"

Kevin told him.

"Ruddy great pigeon," he said.

"Precisely," said the angel.

FOUR

They felt supremely unconvinced. He resembled neither the pictures of Bible stories at school, nor the spangled Christmas cards in Woolworths, nor even the white-sheeted apparitions with paper plates fixed to their heads singing carols in the end-of-term Nativity Play. He was just a man in shabby clothes sitting in an empty London house.

"Ain't you cold?" said Debbie suddenly.

They were all shivering except the stranger. He shook his head and smiled. "But you are," he said. "Why don't you all go home to your dinner, now the snowman's made?"

They looked at each other uncertainly. He seemed friendly enough but grown-ups could be tricky, and this one had after all claimed to represent authority in no mean way.

"The police have gone, if that's what you're worrying about," he said.

"Blimey, how d'you know and all?" said Kevin.

"I saw them go."

"D'you live 'ere?" said Marilyn, looking round.

Again the stranger shook his head and smiled. "Just passing through," he said.

"Why?" said Debbie.

"To see you."

"Howdja know we was in here?"

"When you have lived as long as I have, you know a lot things."

34

They considered him. There were wrinkles at the corners of his eyes, certainly, but now they looked he wasn't all that old, surely — not half as old as Gran had been for instance.

"How old are you, then?" Kevin challenged him.

The stranger appeared to be doing sums on his fingers. "By your reckoning," he said, "give or take a few years for historical miscalculation, I must be round about one thousand, nine hundred and seventy-seven."

The girls giggled. Kevin said severely, "You tell our Dad that. He wouldn't half wash yer mouth out wiv soap and water."

"Whydja want to see us?" said Debbie.

"At last, at last!" said the stranger. "Every question in the wide world except the right one — 'Who are you? Where do you live? How old are you? — every piece of impertinence at your command — *and* you don't believe me when I tell you. I have come, my dear children, to bring you something infinitely precious. I have come to bring you Christmas."

They looked at him expectantly, half-hoping to see a gift-wrapped parcel topped with tinsel and ribbon. But the stranger had nothing but the clothes on his back.

"No you never," said Debbie. "Christmas comes when it's ready. You don't have to bring it."

"Ah! That's just where you're wrong. The twenty-fifth of December, I'll grant you, comes round each year unbidden, but Christmas — that's different. I've handled more Christmasses than you've had hot dinners. I helped bring in the first — in a very junior capacity, of course — and I shall continue to do so until the end of the world. That is why I was created."

Whether they understood him or not, something of what he said struck an answering chord in them all.

Marilyn voiced it. "I'm 'ungry," she said.

"Off you go then," he said. "I told you it's all clear now."

Debbie hesitated. "How long are you stopping?"

"Till the thaw comes and your snowman melts and you don't need me any more."

"Ta-ta, then. C'mon you two. We best go through the front now we're here, to be on the safe side."

She and Marilyn went through the door, pursued anxiously by Kevin. "You can't," he called after them. "I tell you, you can't get out that way. You can't get through the door."

He was right. There was a narrow hall with a chipped stone staircase leading from it and several closed doors. The street door and both windows were boarded up securely. It was dark and already much later than they had meant to be.

Debbie turned back. "Oh come on, then. Let's get back the way we come."

She pushed the door open again, saying to the stranger, "Don't tell no one we — " Then she stopped. The room was as empty as when they had first gone into it.

Outside in the street Kevin said, "He didn't 'arf hop it quick. Think the fuzz is after him an' all?"

His sisters were scornful of such a dramatic notion. Debbie said, "Dare say he were in a hurry to get back to his dinner too. He said he don't live there." She stopped suddenly so that the others turned to look at her. "'Ere! How'd he get out then, eh?"

"Same as us, I s'pose," said Marilyn. "Why?"

"You must be joking," said Debbie. "He's ten times bigger'n what we are. Fatter even than you, Lyn."

"Well, couldn't've been through the front," said

36

Marilyn. "Even we couldn't get out that way."

"We din't try none o' them other doors," Kevin reminded them from the safety of the outside world. "Could be another way through one of them."

"Yeah," said Debbie, "but then we'd've seen him, wouldn't we? I mean, we was in the passage and he'd've 'ad to go right past us to go any other way."

Marilyn shrugged her shoulders. "Must've known 'ow to make that 'ole wider'n what we did," she said.

Debbie followed doubtfully. There was a flaw in this argument but she couldn't quite think what it was. Then, as they rounded the corner by the station it clicked into place. She tugged the belt of Marilyn's coat.

"Listen! Listen! How'd he get *in*, then? He weren't there when we first got inside, and he didn't come in the same way as us, so how'd he get in and out, that's what I'd like to know."

"Blimey!" said Kevin. "'E must be magic!"

They stood staring at each other in the slush of the Saturday shoppers' feet, a little light snow falling unnoticed upon them. An unspoken question hung in the freezing air between them.

"He couldn't be really . . ." began Marilyn.

Kevin's teeth were chattering. "I don't like it," he whimpered. "And I'm froze."

Debbie broke away and began sliding along the pavement. "C'mon, you lot! Whether he is or whether he ain't don't make no difference if we catch it again for being late home."

They were very late, but for some reason which at first they couldn't grasp, they didn't catch it. Their dinner had been kept warm and Mum issued dry clothes without a murmur. But the atmosphere was chilly as the derelict houses. At first they were inclined to think that Auntie Lil must be the trouble. She had evidently won a squatter's victory and was installed in Gran's bedroom with the door locked. From time to time she could be heard coughing, otherwise the children would not have known she was still there. Mum and Dad seemed subdued and absent-minded: Stephen and Carole were getting away with murder, doing all the things that were most forbidden in the ordinary way.

Debbie felt glad when Auntie Lil joined them at tea time: her chatter made the undercurrent of displeasure less awkward.

"Gets dark early now, don't it?" said Auntie Lil, pulling the curtains across the window, and helping herself to two lumps of sugar. "I see you lot's back. Wondered where you was, dinner time. Said to your mum, I said, 'Where's them kids, then? Not at school, surely, Saturday?' " She stirred her tea and watched them thoughtfully. "I sez, 'I hopes they're not getting in any trouble, like Terry.' "

"That will do, Lil," said Mum, quietly. "Stephen, keep yer feet still, and Carole, if you do that once more, you'll go to bed. I mean it!"

The children did not dare ask Auntie Lil to expand on this information, but they looked at her expectantly.

"'Spect you was behaving yerselves, wasn't you?" she said to Debbie. Debbie nodded virtuously. "There you are, Doris, told you so. I said, 'You got good kids, really. You can't grumble at one wrong 'un out of all that lot. You should see some,' I sez."

"If you don't mind," Dad said, turning up the volume, "I'd like to 'ear the news."

There was a blast of fade-out music accompanied by a cackle of laughter from Auntie Lil.

"Think you gonna see yerself on telly then? Think you gonna hear 'em say, 'Family deny knowing whereabouts o' Terry Williamson who weren't home when the coppers come looking for him, dinner time'?"

FIVE

They discussed it in whispers after they had gone to bed that night.

"Think they really come?" said Marilyn. "Or did she just say that?"

"They musta come," said Debbie. "If she was telling lies they wouldn't've took no notice. What'd our Dad turn the telly up for if it weren't to shut her up?"

"But what they want our Terry for?" said Kevin.

"Well I dunno, do I?" said Debbie, crossly. "Better arst him yerself."

"'Spect he ain't licensed that bike of his," said Kevin, knowledgeably.

They were silent for a minute or two. Debbie was reliving the ride on Terry's motor-bike — the noise it made, the power, the sheer size of it. It must have cost a bomb, a machine like that . . . .

"Where did Terry get that bike an' all?" said Kevin suddenly.

Marilyn said, "Fell off the back of a lorry, I daresay," and she giggled.

"Course it din't," said Debbie. "Course our Terry ain't done nuffink like that. He works at a garage, don't he, so he oughter be able to get one cheap."

"OK, then what they come for?" Kevin challenged her.

"I dunno, I tells you!" She sought frantically for some alternative. "Hey, I just remembered summink. Remember how Terry tried to get us away from them

40

houses? Remember how he got when I said we was going in to look round? I bet he's been in there too, like we have, and one of his mates split on him."

"Think he saw that old bloke?" said Marilyn.

Kevin said, "I bet he saw — that other one," he finished lamely.

Debbie was shivering. She pulled the blankets up over her ears and wriggled down into the hollow in the middle of the mattress. A new suspicion presented itself, ten times more unwelcome than the last. Kevin had seen a body in the derelict house; Terry had been there stopping them from going in; the police had come looking for Terry.

"'Ere, I say!" Kevin sat up excitedly. "You don't think — "

Debbie shouted, "Look, knock it off, will you, Kev? You dunno nuffink, so stop blabbing nonsense. Just belt up, will you, and go to sleep!"

"All right! All right! Keep yer hair on," said Kevin. "I ain't done nuffink, have I, Lyn?"

There was a knock on the wall.

"Will you kids just shut up in there? There's others wants to get some sleep even if you don't!"

A sharp frost during the night had spoilt the snow for playing. It was still there in the parks and gardens but as brittle as Christmas cake icing on New Year's Day. Even Kevin gave up when he found it would not stick any more but shattered into little lumps of ice that froze to his hands and hurt them.

"Where we going today then?" he asked his sisters. "Ain't no good for snowballing."

Marilyn also looked at Debbie enquiringly.

"We ain't playing nothink today, you soft kid," said

41

Debbie. "We gotta find Terry."

"Blimey," said Kevin, "you don't think he did an' all, do you?"

Debbie snatched off Kevin's woollen cap and cuffed him. "Course he didn't. But we gotta find him 'cos I gotta know what they did want and no one else ain't gonna tell us."

Marilyn stopped at the street corner. "Where you gonna find him then?"

It was a good question and one which Debbie had been asking herself since waking that morning. "Don't be daft," she said and continued towards the bombed site. Terry had last been seen there; it was possible he might be there again today. Besides, there was nowhere else to look.

Terry was not there. They hung about a bit, sliding on frozen slush and watching two or three other children playing inside the enclosure.

"Our snowman's still there," said Marilyn.

"Yeah," said Debbie. The snowman would remain long after the rest had gone; a little greyer each day, growing smaller, but still a memorial to a marvellous Saturday. Another thought struck her: "Remember what that old bloke said? That he'd hang about as long as our snowman? P'raps he's still in there. He might know where Terry is."

"Why should he?" said Marilyn.

Debbie thought for a minute. The others would laugh at her if she said that angels knew everything. But he had seemed to know things like when it was safe to go home. She brightened suddenly. "Well 'e knows where Cheryl works 'cos I see him there, and she might know where Terry is. C'mon."

The others followed her because they could think of

nothing better to do, and presently all three stood in the cold, bare room.

"Well he ain't in here," said Marilyn, as if she had said so all along.

Debbie tried to hide her disappointment. "He weren't when we first come in last time. We was looking through the window and there he was behind us."

Kevin said, "We better all look out again and pretend we ain't waiting, then p'raps 'e'll come like last time."

They gazed with exaggerated concentration at the snowman till their eyes ached in the white glare, and then they spun round quickly as if to catch the stranger. They repeated this twice, but the room was still empty.

"I'm sick of this," said Kevin. "It's like a silly girls' game and I'm fed up wiv it. Let's go and make a slide somewhere."

"OK, you go," said Debbie. "I'm gonna look for him. I bet he's in this 'ouse somewhere, like last time."

"Oh no you don't," said Kevin when she started for the door.

"Tell you what," said Marilyn, "you go, Deb, and me an' Kev'll wait here in case he comes, and if you don't find him then we'll all go and do summink else."

"OK," said Debbie. She sounded braver than she felt; the house was very dark with most of the windows boarded up. "Whoever sees 'im first shouts."

The hall was just as it had been before: the front door and windows fastened securely and the other three doors shut. She opened one of them. It led to a small room with peeling wallpaper and a large damp patch on the ceiling. She shut it again and opened the one opposite. This was a rather larger room and one of the walls had a jagged hole in it. She went over to investigate. It looked as if something heavy had bashed through a weak place

43

in the structure; there was a lot of plaster lying about and some crumbling brickwork. She thought she could probably just about squeeze through the hole, which presumably led into the next-door house, but it was pitch dark in there, and certainly the stranger could never have got through.

She noticed one other thing about the room; a queer smell over-riding the mustiness of the rest of the building. It was almost as if someone had been burning a bonfire of autumn leaves in there, an aromatic smell which she recognised instantly, but which reminded her of some recent event she couldn't quite place.

She went back into the hall again. There was one other door still untried — the one under the stairs. She opened it more cautiously than the other two, half expecting to find a broom cupboard out of which the stranger might leap, but instead she saw a dark flight of stairs leading to the basement. She peered down it and was rather surprised to see more daylight showing at the bottom than there was in the hall. Then she remembered that the basement windows along the whole row of houses had metal bars in them, so there had been no need to board them up.

It was then that she heard him. He gave a throaty cough followed by an entirely human burp. Debbie turned excitedly back to the others shouting, "I found him! I told you I would! Come on, you two, he's down 'ere, look!"

Even Kevin was reassured enough by her conviction to follow his sisters downstairs. They looked around them. Opposite was the area door, locked, barred and bolted. On the left were what remained of coal cellars, sculleries and the like. On the right was an open door through which had evidently once been the kitchen. They went in, and there, huddled in a corner, coughing, was a boy with the dark beginnings of a beard contrasting sharply with his chalk white face.

"I thought you said you found the old bloke," said Marilyn.

"I thought you was someone else," said Debbie.

"I thought you was dead," said Kevin.

"Sounds like you kids do too much thinking," said the boy. He shifted his position on the floor, screwing up his face with pain. "And what's that supposed to mean?" he added to Kevin.

Kevin didn't answer.

Debbie said, "He come down here Friday and saw you asleep or summink and thought you was dead. Well, you looks queer enough now," she added. "Are you bad?"

The boy closed his eyes and nodded. "Twisted me ankle," he said. "Them stairs is mostly all rotten. What day is it?"

"Sunday," they told him.

The boy whistled softly. "Blimey." He tried to get to his feet. "'Ere, give us a hand." They heaved him into an upright position but he couldn't put any pressure on the ankle. He flopped down again, retching, his pale face greyer than ever. They inspected his leg with interest — there was a red, puffy bulge between his frayed jeans and dirty, canvas shoe.

"Don't it look 'orrible," said Marilyn.

"You got bruises all over," said Debbie. "You been in a fight or summink?"

"Do you mind?" he replied.

"What's yer name?" said Kevin.

The boy hesitated. "Joe," he said.

Debbie studied him thoughtfully. "D'you know our big brother?" she asked. "Terry Williamson?"

45

"Should I?"

"He comes here sometimes, too."

Joe looked at them for a minute and then said, "What for?"

They shrugged their shoulders.

"Same as you, I dare say," said Debbie.

"Tell you what," said the boy. "Could you get me some things?"

"What things?"

"Well, summink to eat for a start. And here — " He opened a large knapsack he had been using as a pillow and brought out a thermos flask. "Fill her up, will you? Nice and strong, plenty of sugar."

"You're shivering," said Debbie.

"Not 'arf." He pulled an old blanket over him and tucked some newspaper in between the folds. "And an old coat'd be good. And a stick. Then when me stummick settles I'll be off."

"Don't want much, do you?" said Marilyn. "Where d'you think we're gonna get all that lot from?"

"Well, what about your place, where you lives, for a start?"

"What about our Mum and Dad, then?" said Kevin. "Can't have nuffink without you tells 'em everything, can you? Just see us, can't you? 'We wants a sangwich for a bloke what's busted his leg in a empty house marked Keep Out, and can we take him your coat, Dad?' "

The girls giggled, but Joe didn't smile.

"Well buy 'em, then," he said. "Don't make no odds to me."

"What with?" They knew that one.

He felt in his pockets but brought his hands out empty. "When you comes back wiv it."

Debbie said, "Bit near Christmas for that, ain't it?"

46

He thought for a moment. Then he said, "Tell you what. I got summink else." He felt again and produced a small object wrapped in a twist of paper.

Debbie said swiftly, "We don't take sweets from blokes as we don't know, do we Lyn?"

"Yeah, sure," he said, "but these ain't ornery sweets. These are summink very very special what'll sell for round two quid or more. Take it to yer brother Terry, or one of 'is mates, not to, like, older people an' them, and whatever you does, don't eat it yerselves."

They looked at each other, the dawn of half understanding in their faces.

"Speed, eh?" said Kevin, knowingly.

"Summink like that, yeah," said Joe.

"Don't look like bennies or thrusters to me," Debbie said, determined not to be duped.

"If you arst me," said Marilyn, "it's just a pep'mint lump or a acid drop."

"Could be anything," said Debbie.

But Joe wasn't listening — he was doubled over laughing, and gasping, "That's rich, that is — acid drops!" Then he had such a bout of coughing no one could talk for a few minutes. When he could speak again he said, "Now scarper, the lot of you. And just bring them things back quick. And look 'ere, if you can get some Aspro or summink for the pain in me ankle, I might find some more of them special sweets."

They took his offering, cynical though they were about its supposed commercial value. After all, he did look dreadfully ill and they had nothing to lose. They knew as well as he did that all the things he wanted were easily obtainable from home with small risk of being missed.

Two hours later they returned with the flask of tea,

47

some cheese sandwiches, an old rug, Gran's walking stick and a handful of Auntie Lil's sleeping pills in a paper bag.

But the way into the derelict house now had several large boards nailed securely across it, and was as impenetrable as all the other locked and bolted doors.

SIX

At first they thought they must have come to the wrong house, but the quantity of footprints making a slushy path to that particular entrance showed that they were not mistaken. They tried to pull the boards off the opening. Nothing would budge.

"Someone done a good job on these," said Kevin. He examined them curiously. One or two had painted letters on them. "FRAG," read Kevin. "That's naughty, that is. Someone din't oughter've wrote that. I bet our Dad'd go mad if he saw that. Wonder what it means?"

"What's 'e wanta shut hisself in for, like that?" said Marilyn. "Don't he want the stuff now we brung it?"

"Are you bonkers?" said Debbie. "It weren't him in there. Them nails is outside. Someone come and done that while we was 'aving our dinner."

"Good job we wasn't in there too," said Kevin.

The full force of what he said hit Debbie smartly. "Cripes! How's he gonna get out, then?"

Marilyn shrugged her shoulders. "Don't reckon as how he will. Bin wasting our time, we 'ave."

"Serve him right," said Kevin righteously, "going in there like that."

"Oh, pack it in, you two!"

Debbie was thinking furiously. "We just got to find Terry now to help us get him out. Well, we can't just leave him there to rot, can we?"

Marilyn pointed to the carrier bag they had brought. "What we gonna do with this lot then? I ain't humpin' it no further."

Kevin said, "You two can share the tea and I'll have them sangwiches."

"Hey! That ain't fair — " began Marilyn.

"Knock it off, will you," said Debbie. "We ain't none of us having it. That's for Joe, that lot is, and no one ain't snitching it."

"Snitching!" said Kevin. "How d'you like that an' all? 'Oo snitched Auntie Lil's tablets while she had her cuppa after dinner then? I saw you, Debra Williamson."

"That ain't snitching," said Debbie indignantly. "She get 'em on the National 'Elf, don't she? Well it ain't snitching if she never pay for 'em, eh?"

And while the other two were still digesting this piece of morality she popped the flask through between the boards into the house, swiftly followed by the packet of sandwiches and the little paper bag of white pills. "There now. When he tries to get out, at least he'll find his dinner waiting."

"You're soft," said Kevin.

"I think she's hard," said Marilyn. "That's me favourite cheese. Wasted. He'll never find it."

Debbie, however, was half way back to the fence. But as she squirmed underneath it she became aware of something just the other side. It was a pair of men's shoes, above which was a pair of trousers. It was too late to retreat; she emerged, while her gaze continued to travel upwards. There was a jacket over the trousers and a man's head on top of that. The face was that of Kevin's class teacher, Mr Webster. The three of them crawled silently out onto the pavement as guiltily as if the whole of Scotland Yard confronted them.

"Judging by your faces," said Mr Webster, "you three have been robbing a bank. May I ask what you have

50

been doing?"

They grinned sheepishly. "We bin making that snow-man and throwing snowballs."

"Can it be possible," he said, "that in two short days you have all completely forgotten how to read?"

"No sir."

"Very well. Can anyone tell me what that notice says?"

"Keep out," they told him in unison, without looking at it.

"And I suppose it never occurred to any of you that it was meant to be obeyed, and for your own safety at that?"

They wriggled uncomfortably and looked at their shoes. This was not the usual Mr Webster at all — everyone's favourite teacher who made jokes about everything.

"All right," he said at last, "we'll forget it this time, but if I catch any of you on the wrong side of that fence again there's going to be real trouble. And just in case any of you should think teachers spend their week-ends in the classroom cupboard and are brought out and dusted over with the blackboard rubber by the cleaning ladies on Monday mornings, just let me warn you that I don't live far from here and might walk through this square any day of the week. Is that clearly understood? Well, Debbie, you look as if you were bursting to say something?"

"Please sir, you looks just like Gary Glitter."

"And you, young lady, can thank your lucky stars you're not standing on school premises in school time. Now buzz off the lot of you, and keep out of trouble if you can."

When they were out of earshot Kevin said, "Now you done it. Now he'll be down on us for the rest of term."

51

"Course he won't," said Debbie. "S'pose I says to our Lyn, 'You don't 'arf look like Raquel Welch,' think she gonna thump me, or do what I wants?"

Kevin took the point. "What we gonna do now, then?"

"We gonna find Terry."

"Ain't it teatime yet?" said Marilyn.

"No it ain't. You only just had dinner."

It was not as simple as it sounded. The police might be after Terry. He might be anywhere. There was only one person who might know where he was and that was Cheryl. They had no idea where to find her either.

"You oughter know," Kevin accused Debbie. "You bin there."

Debbie defended herself. "Yeah, doing a ton 'arf round London wiv me eyes tight shut 'cos of the wind, and Terry's backside blocking the view. You must be joking."

"Well which way'd you go?" said Kevin.

Debbie shook her head. "It seemed like we was going round and round for hours. Mind you, I'd know it if I saw it — it 'ad a orange front to it and it were in a narrow sort of road like Praed Street wiv shops all along both sides."

"Sure it weren't Praed Street?" said Kevin.

"Don't be daft," said Debbie.

"OK, what else did it have?" pursued Kevin. "Any writing or anyfink?"

Debbie thought. It must have had a name, but she couldn't remember seeing anything written up. She could picture the inside perfectly: the steamy windows, the counter and the swing doors through which she had found Cheryl's baby. There had been paintings all over the walls too; she remembered studying them idly while she drank her coke.

"It had animals all round," she said at last.

Kevin exploded with laughter. "Blimey, p'raps you was at the zoo an' all!"

"Pitchers, stupid," said Debbie. "There was a great big cat by me and Terry, all black wiv bright green eyes and his mouth open, grinning. And the walls was orange, and just these great big animals all over black 'cept for their grinning mouths and green eyes."

"What sort of animals?" said Marilyn.

"Don't remember. They was all in different positions like they was dancing, but they all had their mouths like this — " She put two fingers in the corners of her mouth and stretched back her lips, crossing her eyes as she did so.

"Cor — 'ow 'orrible," said Marilyn. "Turn me right off, that would — horses and pigs and things doing that down me neck while I had me tea."

"Who said 'orses and pigs?" said Debbie. "I said cats. Come to think of it, they was all cats."

"Don't make no difference," Marilyn was beginning, when Kevin interrupted: "'Ere! P'raps that's its name — Black Cat Milk Bar or summink!"

His sisters gazed at him with a new respect.

"Where's a phone box?" said Debbie.

They ran to the corner of the nearest shopping street and all crowded into the kiosk together.

"A," said Debbie, opening the top book. "B for Black — here we are, look — oh crumbs! There's pages of 'em!"

It took them ten minutes to crack the code of the directory, and even then there were no Black Cat Milk Bars.

"P'raps they ain't on the phone," suggested Marilyn. They ignored her.

53

"What else could it've bin?" said Debbie. "Dancing Cat? Go-Go Cat?"

"Grinnin' Cat?" said Kevin.

They tried them all with no results.

"Cool Cat," said Debbie, and looked it up under K as well for good measure.

"P'raps it's P for Pussycat you wants," said Marilyn, and she breathed on the window and drew one with her finger.

"Looks just like that old cat wot's hangin' about outside." She added legs, arms, a shopping bag and an umbrella to the picture.

"Give us a butcher's!" Kevin elbowed her to one side and peered out. "She's enough to make a cat laugh," he said.

"That's it!" shouted Debbie suddenly. "I remember seeing it now! The Laughing Cat — that's what it was!"

"Better put yer skates on, then," said Marilyn. "That old basket outside's getting ever so shirty."

Debbie was already thumbing through L-R. "Let her wait," she said, without glancing up. "We was here first."

"Making ever such ugly faces, she is, through the window," reported Marilyn with interest. "Talk about laughing cats an' all."

"I got it!" said Debbie. "Look here — Laughing Cat Snack Bars Ltd., Oxford Street. There you are — what'd I tell you?"

"No you never," Kevin pointed out. "You said a narrow little road more like Praed Street. I heard you."

There was an impatient knock at the door of the kiosk and the would-be caller rattled the handle. "Come on out of there, you kids, I want to make a very important phone call."

Kevin held the door tight shut and said through

clenched teeth, "OK, Deb, I can 'andle this one."

Debbie said, "What'll I do, then? Ring 'em up and arst for Cheryl?"

The woman outside was shouting, "If you don't all come out of there this instant I shall get the police!"

"Who's got some change then?" said Debbie.

"I ain't got none," said Marilyn, quickly.

They both looked at Kevin. Kevin released his grip for one second to defend his pockets and the door burst open.

"Little hooligans!" said the woman. "I know your sort — smashing things up for decent people! Come on! Phone boxes are not for playing in — out, now! I mean it!" She brandished her umbrella dangerously in the confined space.

"'Ere, knock it off, will you!" said Debbie, as they stepped out into the road with as much dignity as possible. "You can 'ave it to take 'ome if you like. We don't want it no more." She turned to the others. "C'mon. If we can't phone 'em, we're going there."

"Why?" said Kevin.

Debbie pressed on towards Marble Arch without replying. It was the only lead they had — their only hope of finding Terry. As they rounded the corner by the cinema Marilyn dug her in the ribs.

"Deb — wait a minute. Deb, d'you really think I looks like Raquel Welch?"

By the time they reached Oxford Circus Marilyn and Kevin were mutinous. At Tottenham Court Road Debbie herself was flagging.

"She would 'ave to choose the longest street in London," she conceded.

"Let's go home," pleaded Marilyn. "Me feet are

55

killing me!"

Debbie almost yielded. They were all tired and it was probably a wild goose chase anyway: certainly this was nothing like the neighbourhood she had come to with Terry. Then she thought of the boy trapped in the house, sick and shivering.

"Tell you what," she said, "give it to that next lot of traffic lights. OK?"

They agreed sullenly, and trudged after her, grumbling.

"What a waste of a Sunday," said Kevin. "I'll bet he's dead anyway by now. I'll bet — 'ere!" He broke off suddenly and pointed across the road. "What's that place?"

It was a bright orange shop front with *Laughing Cat Snack Bar* written in huge black letters over the door. As they crossed over to it Debbie felt less jubilation than she pretended. This was quite definitely not the place she had come to with Terry. But it was open. They went up to the only waitress.

"'Scuse me," said Debbie politely. "Does Cheryl Williamson work here?"

"Who?" said the girl, frowning, as she counted the cups on her tray again.

"Cheryl Williamson."

"No dear," said the girl, and moved away to a corner table.

"It must be right," said Marilyn. "It's got cats all round just like you said."

But it wasn't right. There was a different layout, no swing doors and no Cheryl. They stood there waiting for the waitress to return. When she did, Debbie approached her again, with no very clear idea of what she would say this time.

"Please," she began, "please Miss, can you tell us — "

"Look, can't you see I got work to do?" demanded the girl. "I tell you I never 'eard of 'er. Now 'op it, will you?"

Debbie glared at her. "We'll have three cokes, if you don't mind."

The girl shrugged her shoulders. "In the corner. Serve yerselves and pay at the cash desk."

"It must've bin here," said Kevin as they did so; but the woman at the cash desk had never heard of Cheryl either.

"Sure it's this branch you want?" she said.

"Eh?" said Debbie.

"There's Laughing Cats all over," said the woman, pointing to the back of the cash slip in her hand.

They took it to a table and studied it, new hope mingling with dismay.

"Blimey, there's millions of 'em!" said Marilyn.

Even allowing for gross exaggeration it looked like a Herculean task ahead. To be precise there were nine on the list, each with its address and nearest tube station. Three were in roads they knew and could be eliminated along with the main Oxford Street branch, leaving five possibilities.

"It ain't those two, neither," said Debbie.

"How d'you know?" said Kevin.

"'Cos we went from Victoria when we went to the seaside, and you gotta cross Hyde Park and go round Buckin'am Palace to get there, and I never went that way wiv Terry."

The others were too anxious to whittle down the possibilities to argue with her.

"OK," said Kevin, as Debbie dribbled a line of coke through them with her straw, "that leaves three."

These were, respectively, near South Kensington,

57

Queensway and Kilburn.

"Ain't South Ken," said Debbie. "That's acrost the Park too."

"Gonna finish your coke, Deb?" said Marilyn.

Debbie pushed the rest of hers across the table and said, "Queensway's a bit close to home — we went further'n that. I bet it's Kilburn. C'mon Lyn, stop blowing bubbles will yer, everybody's lookin' at you!"

Forcing Kevin to buy the tickets, they took the Bakerloo Line from Oxford Circus and asked the first person they met when they got off at Kilburn. She looked up and down the street for some time and then said she was sorry, she'd never heard of it. They walked on a little and asked a man with a foreign accent who was a stranger there himself, and a boy on a bicycle who offered to accompany them to the nearest Wimpy Bar. Then they asked an old lady with a very fat dog on a lead, who told them severely that they should take more care of their poor little pussy, it could get run over or stolen for fur gloves. In desperation they stopped a Pakistani who said, Yes, it was the second on the left and then fifty yards along on the right hand side.

They found it easily, with its bright orange paint and black lettering, just like its counterpart in Oxford Street. Debbie vouched for this being the right place without any shadow of doubt, and ran forward this time with no misgivings.

But it was closed.

SEVEN

They all tried the door, as if great strength might reverse the notice hanging in the window, but nothing yielded.

"That's that, then," said Kevin.

"Pack it in now, Deb," Marilyn urged.

But Debbie was already examining the front door of the nearest house.

Kevin warned, "You can't go ringing them bells! You won't 'arf catch it if they hears you!"

"I already rung one of 'em," said Debbie.

"You never!" said Marilyn.

"Says Caretaker, don't it?" Debbie defended herself. "What they get paid for, if it ain't answering bells?" She rang it again. "Get back, you two. If they sees a pack of kids like you lot hanging around they ain't gonna open up at all."

Presently a tired-looking woman in dirty bedroom slippers opened the basement door. She frowned when she saw Debbie, but asked mildly enough, "What is it, dear?"

"Oh please, are you the caretaker?" asked Debbie.

The woman's frown deepened, but she nodded.

"Well, please, d'you know where we can find our sister? She works in there, see, but it's shut and we dunno where she lives."

"Who?" said the woman.

Debbie explained again.

"No dear. I look after this house. You wants the caff, don't you? It's shut all today, see. Be open tomorrow,

59

look — Monday. Always shut Sundays."

"Oh please, it's ever so urgent," begged Debbie.

"It's the manageress you want," said the woman.

Debbie asked how they could find her, but the woman seemed shocked at the very idea. "Oh no, dear. I'm only supposed to bother her on Sundays if it's life or death, like the place has been broke into, or something."

She had begun to retreat when Kevin blurted out, "Blimey, this *is* life or death, innit? He could've snuffed it by now just while we're stood here."

The woman showed a spark of interest. "Someone ill then, dear?"

"Very," said Debbie. "Very, very ill. He's nearly dead. Honest."

They watched her relent and motion them down the area steps. "You better stand on the mat because your feet are all wet."

They stood in a tight group just inside the door and listened to the nearer end of the conversation.

"That you, dear? Yes it's me, dear. No, dear, no fire nor nothink, it's still there! Now, everything's all right, I don't want to worry you, but this is life or death, dear, or as you know I wouldn't worry you on a Sunday. Now then, can you hear me? Is that better? Now then, there's three kids here asking for their sister who works over at your place. Their Dad's ever so ill — " the voice hushed — "Passing away, I think, by the sound of it. What's her name, my dears? Cheryl? Cheryl Williamson, dear. Do you know her address?" There was a long pause, then — "Two one five, Birkenhead Terrace. Thanks ever so much, dear. Sorry to have troubled you. Bye-bye then, dear."

Five minutes later they were walking along the odd

numbers of Birkenhead Terrace.

"Blimey," said Marilyn, "we ain't 'arf done some walking today, and we only just got to forty-three, look."

"What a 'orrible place," said Kevin. "It's all dark and cold and dirty. It's worse than home. It is — honest."

"No one can't help it being dark and cold," said Debbie, who saw this as some sort of criticism of Cheryl.

"Well it's still mucky," said Kevin.

He was right. Old rags of newsprint and sweet-papers were blowing about the gutters, while the half-thawed slush made slimy barriers across every corner. Number two hundred and fifteen seemed like the end of the world, but the terrace stretched on beyond it still. Again, there was a row of bells with little cards beside them. They peered at the names they could decipher in the dim light: there was a Smith, a Carter, three or four that were unpronounceable and the rest were blank. There was no Williamson anywhere.

"Sure this is it?" said Kevin.

Debbie shrugged. "That's what she said."

She rang the nameless bells. Nothing happened.

"Oh come on," said Marilyn. "I'm going 'ome."

"Go on then," said Debbie. She rang again, desperately, and was about to ring all the others as well when a window opened far above them and an angry voice called out, "Who is it?"

They looked up at Cheryl.

Her room was small, cold, unkempt and ugly. They sat in a row on the bed and waited while Cheryl rocked Karen and scolded them tearfully between the spasms of screaming in the carry cot.

"You woke her up, ringing like that. She just gone

off — *just* — after yelling 'arf the day, and you lot have to come and start her off again. I dunno what's the matter with her, I tell you, whether she's teething or it's wind — she throws everythink back up again and then yells for more. I ain't 'ad a decent night's sleep in weeks, and then it's on and on at work trying to get her off without that old cow complaining I ain't looking after the customers. Then I comes home and there's nappies to wash and her to feed and see to, and I'm too done in to eat anythink meself, and then *she* comes up from downstairs, screamin', 'Shut that brat up or I'll have you evicted, I will!' I can't go on, I tell you . . . Shut up, you little so-and-so!" She shook the cot violently and the screams redoubled. "Ah, darlin', I didn't mean it — come to Mum, then — there, there, love, it's all right."

Debbie held out her arms. "Can I hold her, Cheryl? Please!"

She took Karen and rubbed her back as she had seen her own mother do with the younger ones. Almost instantly the noise subsided. Debbie exclaimed joyfully, "Blimey, she remembers her Auntie Deb then! Look, Karen, there's Auntie Lyn and Uncle Kev too."

Marilyn giggled appreciatively, but Kevin was unmoved. "Going on like you was playing dolls or summink," he said scornfully.

"Some doll," said Cheryl. Karen gave a sudden hic-cough and the front of Debbie's coat was covered with a white, sticky fluid. "See what I mean?" said Cheryl.

"It don't 'arf pong," said Marilyn, pulling a face. "Let's go home now, Deb."

"'Ang about," said Debbie impatiently. She turned to Cheryl. "D'you know where we can find Terry?"

Cheryl shook her head. "Weren't it him tell you where I was?"

"No." They told her briefly how they had arrived there.

Cheryl whistled. "There's one thing, you kids don't give up easy." She thought for a moment. "I know the garage where he works. Why d'you want him?"

They glanced at each other uneasily.

"That's our business," said Kevin.

Debbie punched him. "Shut up, Kev." This was no time to antagonise Cheryl. She said, "There's a feller in one of them houses by the bomb site where we play, got stuck, hurt hisself and can't get out. Needs someone a bit strong, like our Terry."

Cheryl looked at them suspiciously. "You oughter call the police, you ought."

"What, and have 'em know we bin in there?" Debbie countered. "Not likely."

"What makes you think Terry'd help anyone?" said Cheryl.

"This feller said he'd give him a — reward."

"How much?"

Debbie looked her straight in the eye. "A fiver. P'raps more."

Cheryl looked bleak. "Lucky old Terry. I'd come and hoik him out meself if it weren't for this one." She paused, considering them. "What are you lot getting out of it then? I don't s'pose you're doing all this for free?"

Debbie drew herself up with dignity. "We ain't as daft as we look," she said.

"Lucky old you too, an' all," said Cheryl. "Don't spend it all at once."

"So you will go and tell Terry, won't you," said Debbie.

"Tell him what?" said Cheryl, taking the now-sleeping Karen and putting her carefully into the cot.

63

"Tell him," said Debbie, "to meet us at the bomb site where we see him last time, after we comes out of school tomorrow, about four."

Cheryl straightened her back suddenly. "Look, I can't go Monday! I got work to do! I got more to do than run errands for a bunch of kids what can't keep out of trouble. Besides, I ain't said I'll go at all yet. I'm the one there don't seem to be nothink in it for, and it's a long way to Terry's garage."

"Please, Cheryl. Please." Debbie felt in her pockets; her fingers closed round the doubtful sweet the boy had given them. Perhaps if she gave it to Cheryl . . . . But then there would be nothing with which to persuade Terry to help. Kevin was fiddling with the few possessions Cheryl had on a shelf by the bed.

"Cor, Cheryl," he said, taking hold of half a jar of jam, "if I was to knock this lot off, think the noise'd wake it up?"

"You just dare." But they knew her well enough to see her weaken.

"What about tomorrow then?" Kevin pushed the jar along until it touched an open tin of beans.

Cheryl tucked a blanket over Karen and said, "I might go Thursday. That's me 'arf day. Now push off and leave me in peace."

But Thursday would be too late.

"No," said Debbie suddenly. "Tomorrow or never. Tell you what, Cheryl, if you get Terry to meet us tomorrow like we said, we'll come an' baby sit for you in the 'olidays. We could come up here most days and take 'er out or sit wiv her when you're busy. Now then."

"Oh blimey, not another weekend like this one — " Kevin began.

"Wrap up," Debbie told him. "You don't 'ave to. In

64

fact I hopes you don't. I don't want you moaning round like you bin today. But I'll come, Cheryl — as often as you want. I'd like it — honest!"

Cheryl was gazing at her. "D'you really mean it?"

"Course I do!"

"Yeah, I think you do. OK then. I'll tell 'im. Well? What you lot still hangin' round for then? Go on — scram!"

They opened the door. The passage was in darkness except for a dim light coming through a half open door next to Cheryl's.

"Hey," said Kevin loudly. "Looks like you got nosey parkers here same as what we got at 'ome."

"Sh!" said Cheryl urgently, but it was too late. A woman stood in the doorway, peering at them.

"Who are you?" she demanded frostily. "What you doin' here?"

"Do you mind?" said Cheryl. "They're me little brothers and sisters, that's all."

"Tell that to the marines. However many more brats have you got round the place, you wicked girl? I know you! I know your sort, I do! I'll 'ave you thrown out of this 'ouse, my girl, see if I don't, and then you'll be back on the streets where you belongs."

She slammed the door and instantly a wail rose from the cot. Cheryl sat down beside it, put her face in her hands and began to sob.

"Cheryl — Cheryl, don't cry," said Debbie. "Look, I'm sure I can quiet her, an' I'm coming again lots of times — "

But Cheryl was shaking her head despairingly. "What's the use if she has me chucked out before then?"

"They can't, Cheryl, honest they can't. Our Dad said so — they can't never get you out if you pays yer rent — "

Cheryl was barely comprehensible. "They can — they can — you don't understand — I can't hardly pay as it is — they keeps telling me I'm gonna lose me job because of her — and I'll never find another where they let me bring her — then they'll take her away from me and put her into care and I'll never see her again — and I'm so tired I can't do no more — I just can't do no more!"

Even Debbie was shocked into silence by this outburst. Marilyn was moved to suggest making her elder sister a cup of tea. Cheryl shook her head.

"I'll have to feed her now and see if that settles her. You lot best get 'ome or you'll have our Mum after you. I knows what that's like." She smiled wanly. "That's why I'm here."

They went cautiously downstairs, more in awe of the other doors than of tripping in the darkness. Outside the street lamps were lit and it was freezing. It was only when they reached the station platform that they spoke again.

"Ooh, my feet!" said Marilyn.

"'Ere, let's sit down," said Debbie. There was only one other passenger on the seat, and he sat in the corner behind his newspaper, so they paid no heed to him.

"Think Terry'll come?" said Kevin.

"Course he will," said Debbie. There was no alternative. Terry just had to be there.

"What if he can't get him out?" said Marilyn.

Kevin said, "Then it's curtains for that Joe, I reckon." And he drew his finger smartly across his throat and crossed his eyes.

Debbie pushed him off the edge of the seat. "Don't talk so daft. Course our Terry'll get him out. Think he's soft or summink?"

The man in the corner put down his newspaper

suddenly. "While I applaud your faith," he said, "I would like at the same time to issue a word of warning, if I may."

They stared at him in amazement.

"Blimey!" said Debbie. "If it ain't our angel! What you doing down here, then?"

"I repeat: I would like to give you a word of warning. Don't trust anyone, however well you think you know them. Understand? Don't . . . trust . . . anybody. Here's your train coming now, look. Goodbye, and good luck to you!"

They all glanced up as the train rattled towards them through the tunnel. When they looked back at each other again, they were alone on the platform.

EIGHT

It was thawing. Icicles dripped from the area railings onto brown, muddy pavements. Marilyn complained of a headache.

"Snowman's still there," said Debbie.

It was the one cheerful aspect of an otherwise dismal Monday morning. The usual parental disapproval over their late return on Sunday evening would have passed over without incident had not Auntie Lil begun to ask several pertinent questions about where they had been, and more particularly, with whom. Their non-answers had at last aroused suspicion and the cross-fire of questions had become increasingly difficult. Eventually Auntie Lil had launched into an in-depth account of what could happen to three naughty kids who roamed the streets of London late on a Sunday. She had just reduced everyone to more or less open-mouthed astonishment when Kevin had been heard to remark, "Cor blimey! That there Auntie, she don't 'arf get her knickers in a twist!"

The girls had been sent to bed too, for sniggering.

Inside the wire-meshed gates of the bombed site bald patches of rubble had emerged through the snow.

"It ain't pretty no more," lamented Marilyn.

Kevin jerked a thumb towards the houses. "Think he's still alive?" Then he added, "'Cos I ain't going in there even wiv our Terry if he ain't."

Debbie calculated. Three days. Well, four really. People didn't eat for much longer than that with flu sometimes. And it was warmer today. "He'll be OK," she pronounced. If Cheryl had bothered. If Terry came. If he could break in . . . . "Come on you two, we're gonna be ever so late, and we don't want to get kept in today."

But they all got out on the dot of half past three, with instructions from the headmaster to hurry home before it began to get dark, because the forecast was bad again. As they crossed the playground the girls saw Kevin chatting to Mr Webster at the entrance.

"Lucky little rat," said Marilyn. "Wasted on him, too." She flicked back a lock of hair and began to walk half an inch taller.

Debbie watched her curiously. "You still fancy Mr Webster then? After how he went on at the bomb site an' all?"

"Yeah! He's dishy. You said so, too."

"C'mon!" Debbie broke into a run. "I'll tell him, shall I?"

Marilyn squealed delightedly and trotted, protesting, after her. But Debbie, with a sidelong glance at her sister, merely bid him a polite "'Bye, sir," as they turned their backs upon school.

"Wait a minute," said Mr Webster, "I'm coming your way. We'll go together, shall we?"

They looked at each other in dismay which he appeared not to notice. He chatted cheerfully about the possibility of another snowfall later, or a more probable downpour to wash away the remains of the slush. The barometer was falling, he said, but the wind seemed to be going round more to the north again. They hardly listened to him. It was raw and cold whatever anyone said, and Joe was still sitting hungrily in that empty basement. Debbie thought of suggesting buying some sweets in the hope that Mr Webster would not wait for them, but what if he

69

followed them into the shop? They would look pretty silly when it was discovered that the weekend had cleaned them out completely.

Kevin suddenly bent down and undid his shoelace. "Got a stone," he said.

The others aided and abetted him, for once, in laboriously shaking first his shoe, then his sock, then supporting him while he put both back on again.

"Don't wait, sir," they urged at frequent intervals.

"It'll take ages doing it up again," Kevin warned him. "Me fingers is froze."

"Here — let me," said Mr Webster. "I've been wearing gloves." He had both Kevin's shoes done up in tight double knots in a trice.

"Blimey!" said Debbie, "he'll be in them till the end of term now."

It was too bad; Mr Webster had never been known to help even the smallest new kid before.

When they came in view of the bombed site the children began to look about anxiously for Terry, but the square was deserted. Debbie was not sure whether she felt more relieved or disappointed. She was trying desperately to think of some kind of delaying tactics when Mr Webster said, "Well, this is where we part company, I think. I go this way, and there's your road. Hurry on home, now, the sky looks terribly black. See you tomorrow."

But he didn't go. He just went on standing there, hands in pockets, quite obviously ensuring that they did not make straight for the forbidden territory. They all said, "'Bye, sir," several times. Then Marilyn thanked him for coming with them. Then Kevin asked him if there would be time to finish their Christmas decorations before the end of term. Then they all said goodbye again, and after that there was nothing more they could do but cross the road and leave him standing there. And still there was no sign of Terry.

As soon as they were out of earshot Kevin said, "Now what?"

"Round the block," said Debbie. "He'll go, soon as he thinks we gone home."

They walked round the next square and came back towards the bombed site. But as they approached for the second time Debbie grabbed them both and ducked behind a corner.

"He's still there," she said.

"What's he doing?" said Marilyn.

"Just stood there, smokin' a fag."

"Have to wait a bit," said Kevin.

They jumped up and down out of sight and looked longingly in at the window of a delicatessen.

"Don't them 'amburgers look smashing," said Marilyn. "I could just do wiv one of them jumbo ones."

"Hey," said Kevin, "why d'you think a elephant's called a jumbo, anyways?"

Marilyn shrugged her shoulders. "So big, I s'pose."

Debbie took another look round the corner. "He's going," she announced. "Walking away. Fed up at last. 'Ang about! Let him get well clear, case he looks round. Oh crumbs! Can you beat it? He's coming back again — just walkin' up and down to keep hisself warm!"

"Well that old bloke did say not to trust no one," Kevin reminded her.

Debbie reflected bitterly on the truth of this. Even if Cheryl had told Terry, Terry hadn't come. And even if Terry came now, a fat lot of use it would be with Mr Webster pacing up and down the fence as effectively as a patrolling guard dog. But Terry wouldn't come now. It

71

was quite dark and must be long after four o'clock. She took one more look along the road. Through the mesh gate the snowman's shapeless mound showed up white against the darkness of the bombed site. Then a black shadow eclipsed it for a moment and moved on, turning at the corner to pass the gate again.

Debbie capitulated. "Oh, come on. I'm goin' home. What you lot keeping me hangin' about like this for?"

And as they started back a bitter little wind sprang up from the north and the first few snowflakes fell silently upon them.

The newspaper headlines were full of it, the television programmes were full of it, the sky still looked full of it too. Far from thawing, the blizzard had of course taken London unawares. Cars had been abandoned, points frozen, trains cancelled — but, the weather men predicted, it was to be short lived and they did not foresee a white Christmas.

The children had been unaccustomed heroes, coming in from Siberia, survivors of an intrepid expedition, with snow on their boots and in their hair. Mum had made them cocoa for tea and even Auntie Lil had admitted she was glad it wasn't her that had to go out in it.

Guiltily at first, Debbie stopped worrying about Joe and was swept along with the general excitement. After all, either he had found a way out somehow by himself, or his sufferings were presumably over by now.

There were no footprints round the bombed site next morning, and no Mr Webster either. They cried out with joy at the fresh white cover like a new coat of paint over their chipped and sooty playground. The snowman had taken on another lease of life, and looked more like the angel sitting in the derelict house than ever.

72

Marilyn sucked a peppermint noisily and remarked that by the time they got a chance to play in it again the snow would probably all have gone.

Kevin sniffed the air. "Where'dja get that from?" he asked her.

Marilyn shrugged her shoulders. "Had 'em ages." She looked at Debbie suddenly. "'Ere, what happened to that sweet that Joe give us?"

Debbie put her hands in her pockets, closing her fingers over a twist of paper. "Why?"

"What we gonna do wiv it, then?"

"Keep it," said Debbie. "You never know."

"Don't be daft," said Kevin, advancing towards her. "That sweet's worth two quid or more — he said so."

"Clear off," said Debbie. "I got it, so I keeps it, see?"

"Well I wants it," said Kevin. "Why should you 'ave it when there's three of us? He give it to me and Lyn too."

"We can't all keep it, it's too small," said Debbie, practically. "And I'm the one what tried to save him, and besides I — " She stopped as a snowball caught her across the mouth. "All right, Kevin Williamson, you arsted for it!"

The others saw her hand dart from her pocket to her mouth, while a small piece of paper fluttered to the ground. Debbie swallowed, ostentatiously.

"*Now* whose is it?" she demanded, triumphantly. "And if anyone still ain't sure I'll put this snowball down their necks!"

Kevin gaped at her in horror. "You ain't never ate it!"

Marilyn began to sniff. "He said don't eat it, for gawdsake! And we might've got two quid for it too!"

"Well I have ate it, ain't I? And I'm glad too. That's what comes of going on like that. It was only one any-

73

way, and people eats 'em in 'andfuls sometimes. And if I dies you'll wish you bin nicer to me, an' serve you right. I hopes I do. And — blimey! Look over there! It's him! It's our Terry coming!"

He appeared from one of the boarded-up entrances and sauntered towards them.

"You should've bin here last night," Debbie told him. "Din't Cheryl tell you?"

Terry stabbed the snow with his foot. "That's kids for you. I leaves me work early and risks getting the sack to come and rescue a bloke I never see in me life and what do I find? There you all are gassing away to some feller for hours on end."

"That ain't no feller," said Kevin, "that's my teacher. We couldn't get rid of him."

"Don't say you was here all the time!" said Debbie. "Where was you?"

Terry pointed to the pillars whence he had just emerged. "'Idin' in there, weren't I? Waitin' for him to go. Then when he gone, you gone too."

"Oh crumbs!" said Debbie. Then: "How'd you know to come back today?"

Terry shrugged. "I knows you goes to school this way. Thought I'd meet you. Now then, where's this bloke?"

"Ain't you gotta go to work today?" said Debbie.

"What, in this? You must be joking. Ain't no cars on the road."

"Well we have," said Marilyn. "Gonna be late as it is."

"OK, you go on then," said Terry. "Don't mind me, will you, sending for me an' all."

"'Ang about," said Debbie. "I'm staying. I'll just write a note from Mum for Lyn to take to the Cow."

She tore a page out of an exercise book and wrote on it in her smallest, neatest handwriting: *Dear miss, I'm*

74

sorry Debra as a bad cold so wo'nt be able to go to school this mornin. Singed Mrs Williamson.

She folded it and gave it to Marilyn for Mrs Cowan. The others went off immediately, evidently relieved at not having to join the rescue party.

"See you later — don't wait!" Debbie called after them. "I'll go home by meself when I'm ready." She turned to Terry. "C'mon."

"Not so fast, young lady, not so fast."

Debbie looked at him enquiringly. She thought he looked smashing with his dark, curly mane of hair and his thick sideburns. A whole day, she thought happily. A whole glorious, snow-filled day off school to spend exploring with Terry. "Well?" she said.

For answer he held out his hand towards her, rubbing the tips of his fingers against his thumb. The message was unmistakable.

"You ain't got him out yet, have you?" she said.

"How do I know he's got it?" said Terry.

"You don't, do you," Debbie agreed. "But you knows you gets nuffink stood here."

"Then 'ow do *you* know he's got it, eh? S'pose he's snuffed it — d'you know he really got it wiv 'im?"

Debbie shivered. Then she said, "Yeah, I seen it. Some of it. I made him show me. I ain't stupid!"

Terry gave her a long, searching look. Then, as if suddenly satisfied, he turned on his heel and started to walk in the opposite direction.

"It ain't that way!" called Debbie. "You gets in 'ere, look!"

Terry ignored her. She ran after him as fast as the snow would allow and pulled his arm. "He's down there," she said. "I'll take you where it's bin nailed up."

He shook her off roughly. "You arsted me to do it,"

75

he said, "now let me get on wiv it my way, will you? I don't carry 'arf a tool bench round wiv me."

After that she followed meekly. He went round to the end of the terrace, vaulted the fence where someone had broken it at a weak place, helped her over and stopped to look round. They were in a little concrete yard bounded by the wall of the last house, some ancient railings and the fence put up by the demolition people. In front of them, leading to the roof, was a wrought iron fire escape marked DANGER in enormous red letters. They went up it holding onto the rusty balustrade, for the snow had made it slippery.

"Don't lean on the outside!" Terry warned. "It's all loose, see."

At the top there was an attic window and a parapet running right along the roof, leaving a narrow passageway connecting all the houses to the fire escape. Terry tried the window, but it was locked, and the panes, though mostly broken, were too small to let anyone through. He started along inside the parapet with Debbie behind him. About half way round he stopped.

"Get down," he said. "The fuzz is out round the square. They'll see us against that roof."

Debbie peeped over and saw two policemen strolling along past the place where the children entered the bombed site. There were no trespassers' footprints on the Tuesday snow, and they walked on, unsuspicious. Debbie and Terry continued, bent double beneath the cover of the parapet, until they came to a block in the passage where an avalanche of slates had slipped off the roof in front of them.

"How much further's the right house?" said Terry.

Debbie looked over. It was hard to tell from so much higher; the angles all looked different. "Not yet, I don't think. Quite a way, maybe."

"Are they still there?"

"Yeah. Down at the end now. Stood looking through the gate."

"Didn't see you, did they?"

"No. They're looking down below."

"We'll 'ave to wait till they gone or they'll see us climb that lot."

Debbie said suddenly, "They come round home looking for you Saturday."

"Who did?"

"The fuzz. I dunno what they wanted. We wasn't there. Auntie Lil tell us they bin."

Terry said something Kevin had once been smacked across the mouth for saying, and fell silent for a while. Then he said: "This bloke down 'ere — you really know he's loaded?"

Debbie hitched up her scarf and her coat collar as far as they would go to cover her ears. "Course I do," she said, without looking at him.

"How much did you see — really *see* — he 'ad? 'Cos I tell you straight, I ain't doing this for peanuts."

Debbie sneezed and used the time it gave her to consider the position. If she guessed short he might give up; if she exaggerated too wildly it would make him suspicious. What she wanted to do was to ask him what he would reckon worth while and double it. Perhaps the time had come to bring out the big ammunition.

"It weren't exactly money," she said through teeth that were chattering with cold.

"What you mean?" he demanded roughly. "If you bin putting me on — "

"Course I ain't!" said Debbie. "It were tablets — I dunno if they was bennies or sleepers — they looked

77

like sweets and they sells for pounds and pounds — he said so."

Terry was staring at her, his face pinched with cold and hostility, a look as much of fear as anger. "Sweets? Oh no!" he was saying. "You little — oh no! Ain't I got enough trouble? That's all I need on top everything, ain't it? Oh blimey!"

As he spoke he began to back away along the parapet on all fours, like a dog that comes face to face with a polecat in a tight corner.

Debbie said, "Stop, Terry! Terry — where you going? Terry! Come back, you can't just go away now and leave me here! Terry!" Her voice broke into a barely audible croak. "He had hundreds — and you can sell 'em, Terry — "

But he had gone.

And it was at that moment that Debbie realised how very peculiar indeed she was feeling.

NINE

There are always rumours in a school: gossip among the boys about the girls; gossip among the girls about the boys — rumours of scandal and petty crime and violence. The children had heard it all before and shrugged most of it off with a "So what?" and a look of unutterable boredom. But lately there had been whispers of a more sinister kind. It was not that they were any more shocking — they seemed if anything rather milder than the average run of gossip — but they were spoken in a jargon of their own which everyone used and no one properly understood.

Marilyn felt lost without Debbie, although she would never have admitted it. Her concentration, poor at best, suffered considerably from wondering about her sister. Several times Mrs Cowan recalled her sharply to the work in hand, and, once, one of the other girls had had to attract her attention with a smart tap on the head with a ruler.

"She's flaked out," said one of them, and it was only then that Marilyn realised they had been talking about her.

"Looks stoned out of her mind if you arst me," Gloria had said, and the others had giggled.

"Always does," said another. "What mind, anyway?" More giggles.

"'Ere, Lyn, what you high on? Must be high on summink to be so dozey."

Marilyn rubbed her head where she could still feel

the edge of the ruler. "Drop dead," she said.

A few minutes later there was a minor disturbance at the end of the room. Marilyn could hear stage whispers travelling from desk to desk. "Bobby Jones . . . joint . . . toilet . . . pass it on!" Her left-hand neighbour passed it to her right-hand neighbour behind Marilyn's back, so she was none the wiser when the sniggers took over. She ignored them, taking no offence as she had never expected to be a link in the whispering chain. But she found herself wishing again that Debbie were there; Debbie would certainly have been in the know, and would have talked about it on the way home.

After lunch she passed Bobby Jones on her way into the classroom. He was standing just inside the door. He seemed to be hesitating between returning to his desk and pushing the wrong way out into the passage again. Marilyn, watching him, thought he didn't look interesting enough to be the subject of a whispering campaign. And at that moment, in front of a large and avidly interested audience, Bobby Jones was violently sick all over the classroom floor.

There was more gossip later — not about Bobby but connected to this incident. Mrs Cowan was trying to explain how people lived in the Middle Ages and a little knot of children just behind Marilyn were discussing something quite else amongst themselves.

"Like them — you know — jubjub things," one was saying. "Bit like jelly tots, and all with fancy names."

"What they taste like?"

"I dunno. I never even saw 'em, only he said they was like that."

"Did he try 'em?"

"Did he 'ave a trip?"

"Nah. Made him sick like Bobby Jones."

Marilyn was listening intently now. Surely they must be talking about the sort of sweet Joe had given them — the sort she had seen Debbie eat that very morning. Joe had been sick too, she remembered. The whispering continued:

"'E said 'e seen someone on a trip, though."

"No! Go on!"

"What 'appened?"

"He said it were 'orrible. Bad trip, see. This bloke thought he could fly — sorta dreamed he were flying, like."

"What's so 'orrible about that?"

"Well 'e weren't in bed, see, and he stepped right out of the window, just like that."

"Was he OK?"

"You must be jokin'! The feller what tell me said he lived on the fourth floor. They had to scrape him off the road same as a cat what's bin run over."

A respectful silence followed this piece of information. Marilyn thought, I hopes that weren't what our Deb ate. Then she took comfort in the fact that Debbie was with Terry who was strong enough to stop her doing anything stupid. And in any case they would be in the basement where there would be nowhere to fall.

Kevin divided all school activities into two unshakable categories: work with his hands was acceptable, work with his head was out. He was therefore delighted when Mr Webster announced a session of carpentry after the mid-morning break, and even more so when he was picked to be one of the chosen few who should help fetch everything required. They followed Mr Webster downstairs, eagerly questioning him.

"Sir, can I start something new?"

"Sir, can I finish mine at home if I don't 'ave time today?"

"What can I make, sir?"

Mr Webster dealt out the jobs.

"Chris, Michael and Peter, you come with me and help carry the tools upstairs. Susan, you go with Kevin and Darren and bring up the wood I've been collecting. Now listen carefully, you three. It's just inside the door where the milk is delivered each morning. You know where that is? Good. Now there's not an awful lot so don't go dropping it about, and — wait — wait! I haven't finished yet. Don't run with it, don't clobber each other or anything else, and watch out for splinters. Right? Off you go then."

Once out of sight they raced each other to the back door of the school. There they saw a few planks of various lengths leaning against the painted stone dado.

"What wood?" said Darren. "Where is it then?"

"He said there weren't much," said Kevin.

The two boys picked up what there was between them.

"What about me?" said Susan. "He said I was to carry some too."

"Well you can't if there ain't none, can you?" said Kevin.

"If we drops any," said Darren, "you can have it. OK? C'mon Kev."

Susan followed, empty handed, biting back tears of frustrated women's lib. She was barely through the classroom door before she unfurled her banner loudly to Mr Webster.

"Sir, it ain't fair! You said I was to help them, din't you? Well they carried it all and I hadn't none — *and* they ran all the way — and I hopes they got splinters!"

"That will do, Susan," said Mr Webster wearily.

"They couldn't have carried it all anyway. Come on, you boys, where's the rest of it?"

But they turned to him the genuine blankness of innocence.

"D'you really mean you brought all there was?"

There were eager volunteers to go and have another look. Mr Webster held up his hand for silence.

"I'll make a few inquiries in the dinner hour," he promised, "but it looks as if it's been pinched, I'm afraid. Sorry, everybody; my fault, I suppose, for putting it too near the door in temptation's way. I stood it there to dry before the weekend and never checked to see it was still there. Well, there it is, timber's expensive stuff and I must've made it a bit too easy for someone. Let that be a lesson to us all. As usual it's a case of everyone having to suffer for one person's misdeeds. I'm afraid it means no one can start anything new this term, but we'll try and scrape up enough to finish what's been started."

There was a good deal of righteous grumbling about the kind of person who'd nick innocent school kids' wood that had been specially put by for them, but on the whole the shortage had a good effect on the class. Everyone made use of what wood there was with more than usual enthusiasm. Careless waste incurred the wrath of the whole class as well as Mr Webster, resulting in greater accuracy and industry than was usually seen in weeks of work.

Kevin was making a plate-rack. He lacked one piece of wood to go across the back to prevent the plates sliding through. Mr Webster allocated him a bit when he collected his work, and he was delighted to find when he got back to his place that it was about an inch too long for his purposes. That meant a turn with the saw. He reversed it to mark the right length with a pencil — and then he stopped.

There was something written on the wood in faint black ink: the letters ILE had been stencilled on in capitals that didn't quite meet at the corners. Kevin had seen letters like that very recently, on identical pieces of wood.

At dinner time when everything had been packed away again, Mr Webster once more held up a hand for silence.

"Incidentally," he said, "I've been taking it for granted that the wood was removed from the school, but of course I don't know this for certain. If any of you sees any sign of it around the place I want you to come and tell me privately at the end of school. No one is to accuse anyone else of pinching it, however suspicious the circumstances. Remember, stealing is a pretty serious thing, so just come and tell me quietly if you think you've found it, and don't go accusing anyone."

Kevin paid little attention to the afternoon classes. Like Marilyn, he wished Debbie were there: Debbie would have known what to do. He wriggled to and fro in his seat, uncertain which of two courses of action would make him the bigger traitor. Instinct told him Debbie would have insisted on his silence; on the other hand his whole form would be behind him if he talked. Besides, there were other advantages in letting on — advantages that even Debbie would appreciate: presumably Mr Webster would come and reclaim the wood, and then, if Terry had not come up to scratch, Joe would still be released after all.

When half past three came, Kevin strolled nonchalantly up to Mr Webster's desk, his mind made up. He stood waiting, hands in pockets while Mr Webster tidied everything away and said goodbye to the others one by one. When he had finished they were alone in the classroom.

Mr Webster looked up. "Well Kevin, what can I do for you?"

"I knows where it is."

"I take it you mean the carpentry wood. Well, where is it?"

"In the bomb site, nailed acrost one of them doors to the houses."

"Oh. Are you sure?"

"Well — it looked like it — from where we was, that is."

"One piece of wood looks very much like another from that distance, and as far as I remember there are a good many boards nailed to those houses. What makes you so sure it's the same wood?"

Kevin fell right in. "Well sir, that uvver wood had letters on it, and that bit you give me today had more letters on it, same as what that uvver lot had."

"Hm. Nothing the matter with your eyesight, anyhow."

"No sir."

"Well, thank you for telling me, Kevin. Unfortunately there's not a lot I can do about it. You know yourself that's forbidden territory."

Kevin was shocked. "Sir — you ain't just gonna leave it there, are you? Ain't you gonna tell the police or summink? Someone's stole that wood, didn't they? You said yourself, that's serious."

"So is trespassing, Kevin. Especially on dangerous ground. Do you really want me to tell the police — everything?"

It always came back to the same in the end. Kevin felt a sudden upsurge of anger and frustration against a system that always seemed to work in opposition to him.

"The fuzz ain't no flippin' good anyway. They don't know the 'arf of what goes on in them houses."

He started to walk to the door but Mr Webster called him back again.

"Stop a minute. What does go on inside those houses?"

"Nuffink."

Too late, Kevin realised he had said too much. He shut his mouth with a snap, his face as unyielding as a prison wall. They looked at each other for a few moments in silence. Kevin's expression made it obvious that there was nothing more to be learnt. You could keep him there till the same time tomorrow, you could starve him, you could beat him, but he would remain as uncommunicative as he chose.

Mr Webster sighed. "Listen, Kevin. Come back here and sit down for a minute. You're no fool and you deserve an honest deal. I think the police probably know a lot more than they let on."

The barriers of silence, though still within reach, were temporarily laid aside.

"Then why don't they do summink about it?"

Mr Webster leant forward, resting his elbows on the desk, his chin on his hands. "Look here: put it this way, then. Suppose you're a large baddie at the top of the school and you want something belonging to someone else. How do you set about getting it?"

"Nick it. No — 'ang about. If I'm a big kid I'll make one of them littl'uns nick it for me."

"Why?"

"Stands to reason, don't it. If he cops it he gets done over for it, not me."

"But what if he squeals?"

"Smash his face in, wouldn't I. Duff 'im up proper, I would. His own mum wouldn't know him, I tell you. He won't squeal."

Mr Webster looked startled. "Sometimes, Kevin, I'm

extremely glad I'm still bigger than any of you. But seriously, I think you've hit on the right answer. You see — put yourself in the position of the authorities now. Say you know what's going on, are you going to arrest the little chap pulling the job? He's not the real culprit, and if you blow the whole thing wide open the big blokes make off quickly and you don't catch the people who are really doing the harm. Do you understand?"

"Yeah. But how d'you ever catch anyone then?"

"I think very often the police have to play a waiting game. They have to lie low and pretend they haven't noticed until sooner or later the chaps they really want make a mistake and give themselves away. Then the cops jump in and catch the right ones. So you see, if the general public interfere they can bust the set-up too soon and frighten off the big baddies and wreck everything for the police. Now do you see why I'm so keen that you should all keep away from that bombed site?"

Kevin saw. His eyes were round with excitement.

"Crumbs — yeah! Me an' Lyn best get off home quick and tell our Deb."

"Debbie? Wasn't she in school today?"

The barriers of silence returned immediately to Kevin's expression. "She got a cold," he said shortly, and then added defensively, "We brung a note from Mum din't we?"

Mr Webster rumpled his hair playfully. "OK, Kevin, I've twisted your arm enough for one day. You get off home, and Kevin — think about what I've been saying, won't you?"

Debbie was shivering. Her ears sang, her legs ached and her nose ran. She looked helplessly along the roof and called out again, "Terry!" At least, her mouth formed the word but her throat only croaked the sound. Very shakily she went back to the fire escape. He had gone.

She sat there for several minutes unable to summon the energy needed to get down the slippery staircase. Her eyes blurred and the steps seemed to merge and then spring apart again when she looked down at them.

Suddenly she stiffened. There in the road below were three familiar figures: a large one with a pushchair containing two much smaller ones. Debbie edged back a little, trying to hide behind the corner of the roof, and knocked a wedge of snow off the parapet down into the street. The larger of the two small figures looked up and pointed.

"Look Mum, there's our Deb up there on that roof."

"Ain't I tell you enough times not to tell lies, Stephen? Debbie's in school."

The smaller figure piped up, "Hullo, Deb, I can see you!"

Then at last the largest one turned round and looked up at where they were pointing.

"Sakes alive, it is her, too! Debra Williamson, what the flippin' 'ell d'you think yer doing up there, then? Come down off of that roof *at once*, my girl, or I'll thrash the livin' daylights out of you, so 'elp me I will!"

TEN

The funny thing about Mum was that however angry she
might be, when anyone was ill that person immediately
became a saint and a hero. Debbie had no need to lay
on the agony any thicker than it really was: one or two
croaks that would have done justice to a geriatric chain
smoker, and she was tucked up in bed with a hot water
bottle, steaming drinks and aspirin. Thankfully, she
succumbed to the full invalid treatment, and as the
shivering gave way to a warm desire for sleep she whispered hoarsely, "That don't 'arf feel good, Mum."

"There you are then, pet. I'll just draw them curtains
acrost and keep the light out, and you 'ave a nice lay
down till dinner time."

Debbie did. In fact she slept till four when the others
came home from school.

"What you doing here?" Kevin wanted to know. "I
thought you was only kidding."

"Was it that sweet you ate, Deb?" said Marilyn. "Did
it make you sick — and did you get that Joe out OK?"

"Get lost," said Debbie, turning her face to the wall.

"Come on out of there, Marilyn and Kevin!" called
Mum from the kitchen. "You dunno what she might 'ave,
and I don't want the lot of you down wiv it. Come and
get your tea."

Debbie felt much better. Even so, recovery would start
the others asking questions again and, worse, there
would be the little matter of the rooftop to be thrashed
out when Dad came home. She decided she could do with

twenty-four hours convalescence before facing the wrath to come. It was boring to lie there doing nothing, but she resisted the temptation to ask for something to amuse her, or to show interest in more than one slice of bread and butter at tea time. Conscientiously she shut her eyes whenever anyone came to the door, and eventually she drifted off into another doze which carried her safely through Dad's homecoming, the others' bedtime, and indeed most of the night.

Next morning Marilyn brought her breakfast in bed. "Cor, you din't 'arf snore last night," she remarked.

"Made a change from listening to you, then," Debbie retorted.

"Mum says don't spill it."

"Spill it? There ain't hardly enough there to spill. That all I'm getting?"

"It's all I'm bringing you," said Marilyn. "Make us late, you will, running in and out wiv trays."

"Mum!" Debbie called out, "Mum, can I get up now and go to school?" She managed to follow the request with a bark that raked her guts.

"No, you can NOT," Mum reassured her, as predicted. "'Ere, wait a bit, you two, I better write a note for you to take."

A few minutes later Marilyn crept in with an almost exact replica of the one Mrs Cowan had received the day before.

"She don't need anuvver," she whispered.

Luckily it was undated, and might come in handy on another occasion. Accordingly, they filed it.

"Come on Marilyn, what you doing in there?" shouted Mum.

"Looking for me shoes!"

"You got 'em on yer plates, you silly twit," said

Debbie from the safety of her sick bed.

"Mum! Mum, I feels ever so queer." That was Kevin's voice. "Mum, I think I got what Debbie got."

"You'll get more'n you bargain for in a minute, my boy, unless you gets off to school this instant!"

Presently the front door slammed, the voices ceased and the flat became strangely quiet. Debbie gave up any pretence at being ill. She got up and put on a pair of slippers and her school jersey over her pyjamas, and sidled into the kitchen. Mum and Auntie Lil were sitting at the table drinking tea, while Stephen and Carole messed about with the remains of their breakfasts.

"Thought you was s'posed to be ill," remarked Auntie Lil.

Rather to her own surprise Debbie leaned against Mum and put her arms round her.

"Ah bless her, she's better today, ain't you, duck?"

Auntie Lil looked sceptical. "Kids today are more lucky'n what we were, ain't they, Doris? We never got the day off of work once we was better."

Debbie treated her to a fair imitation of a watch dog greeting night prowlers.

"See?" said Mum, with equal triumph. "I'll get you some mixture, pet; that'll loosen it."

Later, while the little ones watched the morning television programmes, Mum did some cooking and Debbie was allowed to help. She rolled out the suet for Dad's favourite pudding that night and spread the syrup on it.

"Lick the spoon," said Mum. "Ease yer throat, that will."

"Sweeten him up too," said Auntie Lil, voicing Debbie's own thoughts. "P'raps he won't be quite so flippin' mad when 'e 'ears where you was found an' all yesterday."

91

Debbie might have been bored in bed, but she had not been idle. "There was this poor little cat up there, see, miaowing and miaowing, musta bin starving, I reckon, and couldn't get down. Ever so thin it was, and poorly looking. I just had to help it, din't I?"

Auntie Lil pursed her lips and shook her head, but Mum said stoutly that their Debra always had been the one for animals — soft about 'em, she was.

"She ain't soft," said Auntie Lil darkly.

Debbie reckoned it was her day as far as Mum was concerned, and decided to press her advantage.

"Mum?"

"Yes, love. Damp the edges, look, or it'll all fall apart."

"Mum — our Terry don't come home no more now, do he?"

"No, dear."

Mum turned away quickly and ran the tap full blast into the sink. Debbie waited while she looked out the largest saucepan, half filled it, set it on the gas and wrapped the pudding in tin foil. Only then did she turn off the water.

"Mum," said Debbie. "Mum, why don't our Terry come home no more?"

There was a long pause, then Mum said evenly, "Terry's grown up now, see. He got his own friends — don't need to come here for nothing, do he?"

"No, but I was just thinking — wouldn't it be nice if our Terry was to come 'ome for Christmas? You know, just Christmas day, like."

Mum gave a sigh and dropped the silver parcel into the boiling water, replacing the lid with an air of finality. "Yeah, well you better arst 'im, then. You sees 'im more'n what I do these days, it seems."

Debbie said hesitantly, "If I was to arst him, and he come, would it — I mean, would you — " She stopped, uncertain how to say what she wanted.

"She means," said Auntie Lil, "would you kiss 'im or belt 'im one?"

Debbie kept quiet; it was exactly what she did mean.

"He's my son, ain't he? What'd I want to belt him one for? He can do as he likes for all I care. Free country, innit?"

So far so good, and Mum might never be in such an agreeable frame of mind again. Debbie took a deep breath. "What about Cheryl, then? Can she come too?"

For answer Mum turned the tap on with such force that the water splashed up and drenched everyone. Auntie Lil shook herself like a dog after a swim and remarked, "'Ere, give over, Doris, will you, you'll 'ave us all on the run in a minute with that tap going like that."

"Can she, Mum?" Debbie persisted.

"I don't care where you run to!" shouted Mum. "I've had just about enough of you two this morning! I will NOT turn the water off till I finished using it, and if you don't like it you can get the 'ell out of here back where you come from. And as for you, my girl, I'm just about sick to death of you and your questions — makes me dizzy, you do — so you can just get back to bed where you belongs, because if you catches pneumonia through racing round with 'ardly nothink on and that cough you got, don't arst me to nurse you no more, because I ain't gonna!"

Debbie had recovered.

In school Mr Webster was glaring at his class with mock ferocity. "If," he said, "IF this noisy bunch of ne'er-do-wells in the front here would settle down and

93

do as they've been told, the whole lot of you would stand a much better chance of being taken to the Science Museum this afternoon."

In the sudden silence that followed he dropped his voice to a near whisper. "And I may say that until this very moment your chances of getting there were practically nil. Now then, as I was saying . . ."

Kevin abandoned the fight he had been having with the boy next to him. He was longing to know whether the Science Museum was the place with all the stuffed animals or the one where you turned handles and the wheels went round and things happened. He hoped very much that it was the latter; the animals didn't get fed or even make an interesting noise, and besides, it was only the girls who preferred them . . . .

He came to when the bell went at dinner time, to hear Mr Webster say, "And that is just what we are going to see happening this afternoon, amongst other things, I hope."

Kevin rather wished he had heard what it was they were going to see happen, but it had never entered his head to listen to what Mr Webster had been saying. At any rate, it looked like being the right museum — nothing happened in that stuffed zoo place.

There were sausages for dinner—usually Debbie's favourite, but somehow today she could not summon much enthusiasm for them. She sat at the kitchen table with Mum and Auntie Lil while the little ones ran around, unchecked, with their bibs on, and every time she coughed there were black looks from both grown-ups. She was glad when the meal was over, even though it was to be followed by a rest on her bed for the afternoon. She didn't really feel fit for anything else, especially

94

now that Mum was back in fighting form. Auntie Lil had been given immediate notice to quit twice, but still sat happily smoking and sucking her teeth in the kitchen. Finally Mum announced that she was taking Stephen and Carole to see Father Christmas at Selfridges, and Debbie guessed that this was less a treat for the little ones than an opportunity of getting out of the flat for a bit.

Mum cleared up, changed herself and the children and issued instructions as she did so.

"Don't wait if we're not back. I'll probably give 'em tea there if they behaves theirselves, and do a bit of shopping while I'm at it. Tell Marilyn to get it: she's quite old enough to do a bit to help now. And look after Dad — hold still, Stephen, I'm trying to put yer shoes on, look — no, don't do that to Carole or I won't take you — stop that noise at once, Carole, it weren't as bad as that. And just you stop that coughin', Debbie, you'll only make yer throat worse, going on like that."

Eventually the door slammed and they were gone.

"Well, that's that, then," said Auntie Lil. "Peace for a bit. Think I'll 'ave a little lay down meself. Me head's splitting wiv her going on like that. I'll take some of me tablets and see what that do."

Debbie went thankfully to her own bed. She kicked off her slippers and slid in under the blankets, wondering as she did so what Auntie Lil was making such a fuss about now. There was a great creaking of floor boards and muttering, and she could hear cupboards being opened and banged shut again. Then her own door flew open and Auntie Lil appeared at her bedside.

"You kids bin in my room, eh?"

Debbie, only half awake, frowned and shook her head.

"Well someone's bin at me tablets. I 'ad nearly a full

95

bottle and now there's 'ardly more'n a 'andful. What's 'appened to 'em then, that's what I wants to know."

Debbie, now fully alert, shook her head again and shut her eyes tightly. She was surprised the theft had been spotted: Auntie Lil must be sharper than they thought; they hadn't taken all that many to Joe.

"Well someone's 'ad 'em. Don't hardly fink Doris or Les would, and them babies ain't big enough to reach."

She sniffed around the children's bedroom for a minute or two — even feeling under Kevin's mattress, Debbie observed through half-closed eyes — but there was little enough furniture in which to conceal anything, and she soon shuffled off again, muttering to herself. More cupboards and drawers could be heard opening and shutting. Presently she showed up outside Debbie's room again — she had left the door ajar and Debbie could just see her moving about in the dim little hallway. She was looking through the pockets of Debbie's school mac hanging up by the front door, and murmuring, "If I finds 'em there won't 'arf be trouble. I'll bet anyfink it's one of them kids — all the same these days, take things soon as look at 'em, they do."

Debbie was not particularly worried. The missing tablets were well away from the premises, leaving no incriminating evidence. Auntie Lil was pulling out the contents of her pockets piece by piece, declaiming an inventory as she did so.

"'Andkerchief — grubby, too; 'air clips, broke, that one is, no wonder she never got none to use; dunno what that is, summink they does at school I s'pose. Oh my good gawd — liquorish! Never could bear the stuff. Ugh! Don't 'arf pong — bin sucked too. 'Ere — what's this then — some sorta sweet — "

Debbie opened her eyes wide, her heart suddenly

96

thumping. The sweet Joe had given them! She had slipped it into her pocket the day before, after pretending to eat it, and had completely forgotten it was there.

"Only one," Auntie Lil was saying. "Serve 'er right if I was to 'ave it, seeing as they nicked me tablets. 'Ope it's peppermint — them bangers is repeating on me summink chronic."

With that she popped the sweet into her mouth and trundled off to her bed, still muttering.

Mr Webster's class had been divided into two groups for the museum trip: half going with Mr Webster and half with Miss Drake, a trainee teacher of extreme youth and newness.

"Come along, come along now," said Mr Webster. "It doesn't matter who goes in which lot. No, look here, I'm not having all you boys in one group, everybody gets too wild and rough in the train." He divided them again and counted the heads as they walked out of the building. "Right. Thirty-seven altogether. You all set, Miss Drake? OK, see you at Paddington, and it's the Circle Line, remember, to South Kensington."

The two groups travelled together on the outward journey as the train was reasonably empty at that time of day.

"On the return journey," Mr Webster decreed, "we'll stagger it a bit. It's not fair to fill the middle of the train with school kids when people are trying to get home."

The crocodile wound chattering along the covered way from South Kensington and emerged at the Science Museum. For the next hour or so there was busy contentment punctuated by questions. Kevin was blissful, the more so because most of the girls were lamenting

97

the absence of lions and elephants and "that great huge wossname what has a whole room to hisself."

At three o'clock they gathered at the exit. Mr Webster divided them again and sent the first lot off with Miss Drake, then counted the remaining heads and ushered them out of the door. Kevin found himself standing beside Mr Webster with a restraining hand on his shoulder.

"Don't push! No pushing please! Everybody go sensibly now."

The pressure was removed and Kevin walked out with the last few people. Mr Webster stayed at the back talking to the children there as they retraced their footsteps to the station.

As they approached the last bend in the subway there were some youths lolling against the wall. One of them sat on the ground playing a guitar and singing softly to its accompaniment; he had a bandage round one ankle and the children stared at him as they walked carefully past his feet. Kevin looked too: the frayed jeans were familiar, so also the pale, bearded face.

Mr Webster stepped in front of Kevin at that moment to tell someone to keep going, so nobody noticed him pause at the end of the line.

"Hello, Kevin," said the boy in a low voice. "Remember me?"

"Yeah," said Kevin. "Yeah. You got out, then."

"Sure."

He looked towards the retreating crocodile and Kevin glanced up too, in time to see the tail of it disappear round the corner.

"Right-o, you two," said the boy softly, and Kevin found his arms suddenly pinned behind his back, while a piece of rough cloth was tied tightly round his mouth.

Debbie had taken a fatalistic attitude to Auntie Lil's scoffing Joe's sweet. She didn't really believe that one tablet of anything could do you much harm. If it could, well Auntie Lil must take the consequences. She was unlikely to confess where she had found it, and in any case was more likely to blame any resultant illness on the sausages. Debbie began to doze.

Half an hour later she was snatched back to wakefulness by a peculiar noise. For a while she thought it must be a dog whimpering, but pets were not allowed in any of the flats and the sound came from somewhere nearer than the street. She lay and listened for a little, decided it must be somebody's transistor in an adjoining house and once more pulled the blankets up over her ears. But the whining grew louder and more urgent, until Debbie could no longer shut out the sound with bedclothes or anything else. She got up and went to the window, but it was impossible to see much since Dad had screwed down the fastening. In any case the sound was not so clear there; she had heard it more distinctly with her head by the door. She went into the passage and listened by the kitchen. There was no doubt the noise was coming from Auntie Lil's room.

Debbie knocked quietly and called out, "Are you OK, Auntie?"

The noise stopped but there was no reply. Debbie listened intently for a few seconds and then called again, "Auntie! You OK?"

In the silence that followed Debbie began to wonder about the sweet Auntie Lil had eaten. What if the noise she had heard had been Auntie Lil stoned out of her mind? Debbie knocked again, turning the handle of the door. It was not locked; she opened it cautiously, half afraid to look inside the room.

The bed was empty. Auntie Lil sat hunched in Gran's old easy chair, her fingers gripping the arms tightly. Her eyes, wide open, stared vacantly at the opposite wall. Debbie came a little closer.

"Auntie — " she began.

"Don't move!" Auntie Lil interrupted urgently, her lips barely forming the words.

Debbie froze, the backs of her hands suddenly prickling with fear.

"The biggest one is just behind you," said Auntie Lil softly.

"Biggest what?" whispered Debbie.

"Stand quite still," said Auntie Lil between clenched teeth, "I fink it's coming this way again."

Mice? wondered Debbie. Cockroaches? "What is it, Auntie?"

"It's big as a rat," said Auntie Lil, "wiv legs — lots and lots of great hairy legs, and slimy eyes." She gave a loud gasp and tucked her feet up under her in the chair. "It's running! It's running this way! LOOK OUT!"

Burying her face in her hands, Auntie Lil gave a long, thin, shrill, mind-bending scream.

ELEVEN

Debbie jumped round with a startled cry — and saw dirty, ochre wallpaper, the chipped wainscot and the frayed edge of a very worn carpet.

"There ain't nuffink there, Auntie," she said.

Auntie Lil still sat with her hands over her face, moaning. Debbie recognised the same sound that had woken her, and went over to the little hunched figure. Very gently she laid a hand on one skinny arm and said, "It's OK, Auntie, there ain't nuffink there, look."

Auntie Lil winced at her touch, but the moaning stopped.

"They're there all right. P'raps you don't see 'em, but they're in here somewheres. I seen 'em — dozens on 'em — sitting on the walls, they was, and crawling on the floor."

Debbie forced herself to take another look. What was that moving over there? Could it be the legs or whiskers of something, or was it just threads of carpet waving in the draught under the door? A black mark on the wall caught her eye and she started. Surely it slid down a little . . . . No, she knew that place; it was only a chip in the plaster and the spidery lines were cracks running from it. But maybe what she had just seen move was something alive inside it . . . . Those whiskers on the floor still stirred a little; she tiptoed towards them, peering anxiously, her heart drumming. Bare canvas threads lifted slightly in the movement of the air and subsided onto dusty boards again. Debbie put out a bold hand and

101

touched them: dry, still, reassuring matting and wood. With some relief she said cheerfully, "I knows what you seen, Auntie. It did look like spiders for a minute, but it's only the edge of the carpet where it's gone through."

Auntie Lil looked up with wild, unseeing eyes and pointed to the floor by Debbie's feet. "What's that then?" she demanded. "What's that then, I'd like to know."

"What's what? There ain't nuffink here."

"*That*! Oh gawd, it's seen me — don't it run then! All its legs going like windmills — no! NO! Not over here, oh no — it's gone under me bed — I'll never get a wink tonight!"

She grabbed an umbrella from the corner and started poking frantically under the furniture. "I got one!" she screamed, "I cracked its shell! Ugh! It's all green inside — oh gawd, it's not dead, it's still coming — all that pus, it must be poison through and through — all oozing green stuff down them furry legs." She banged the umbrella violently: there was a sharp crack and the handle broke off cleanly and shot into the corner.

"I got it!" yelled Auntie Lil. "I broke its leg! Yah! You can't run at me now, can you! *Now* come for me and see what I'll do to the rest of you, you great hairy monster! I'll larn you — see if I don't!" She looked suddenly at the broken umbrella in her hand and dropped it as if it had bitten her.

"Bats!" she shrieked. "Great tatty black wings and stinking mouths, they got. Look at 'em flapping around! They're all over me, look!" She plucked at her clothes and beat wildly at the air. "They're walking up me legs! They're getting in me hair! There's one gorn down me neck! Aaah!!"

Debbie, frightened half out of her wits, tried to pull

herself together and think what she should do.

"It's OK, Auntie Lil," she said as calmly as possible.
"It's OK, really. There ain't no spiders or nuffink, honest
there ain't. Don't worry, Auntie, just lay on your bed
like you was going to, and I'll — and I'll fetch Mum, see,
and you have a nice lay down and you won't see no
more naughty spiders, look."

She took hold of Auntie Lil's thin brown wrist. Auntie
Lil resisted with the strength of panic, screaming that
they had got her, furry ones with claws and feelers,
squirming in her clothes and crawling down her
throat. . . . The screams turned to choking and the
choking to a weary, anguished sobbing.

Debbie took advantage of being able to make herself
heard and put all the firmness she could manage into her
voice. "Come on now, Auntie, we've had enough of this
carry on; you just get into bed like a good girl, see, and
stop it." The sobbing began to escalate into a steady wail
again. "Stop it!" shouted Debbie, stamping her foot and
sounding more like Mum every minute. "Stop it at once,
I say, or you'll get a good 'iding! You wait till Dad gets
home and I tells him!"

If only he would, she thought, or Mum and the kids —
or even the others from school would be better than no
one.

Once more the terrible screaming began to take over:
"I'm crawlin' wiv 'em — maggoty, all maggoty with
grubs — they got worms coming out all over 'em — all
wriggling and squirming into me — "

"Shut up, I tells you!" shouted Debbie furiously, and
as the screaming redoubled she turned on Auntie Lil
and boxed her ears as hard as she could go. Auntie Lil
cringed, then her face crumpled and the crying began
again — not the choked, terrified sobbing Debbie had

103

heard before, but a shrill childish grizzle that contrasted grotesquely with the wrinkled face and throat from which it came.

"I bin a good girl, Mum," Auntie Lil whined, and Debbie turned cold at the high, wheedling voice she heard. "Me not naughty, Mum — Mum not hurt Lil! Lil not naughty no more!"

She leaned forward and grabbed Debbie's dress, screwing up her eyes and leering in her face. Debbie leaped back with a cry of fear and disgust, and Auntie Lil covered her face and began to wail like Carole. "Mum not shut Lil in cupboard! There's spiders in that cupboard! Lil don't like spiders — no, Mum, no!"

There was not a shadow of doubt in Debbie's mind: Auntie Lil had gone stark, staring, raving mad. Debbie gazed at her for a moment or two, numb with horror, then she darted to the door, snatching the key from it, with the intention of locking Auntie Lil in her room while she went to get help. Auntie Lil, however, was too quick for her; she caught hold of Debbie's arm in a grip like pincers, clawing and scratching at the hand that held the key.

"Stop it, Lil, stop it, I tells you!" shouted Debbie, hiding her terror behind her most authoritative voice. But the key was no longer in her hand, and blood was running down her fingers and up her sleeve. Auntie Lil grinned triumphantly between little clusters of bilious yellow bubbles that dribbled from the corners of her mouth into the creases of her chin.

"Give it me!" Debbie shouted, tears of panic rising in her throat. "Give it me, you naughty, naughty girl, or I'll — I'll lock you in that cupboard, I will, along of all them spiders and creepy-crawlies!"

Auntie Lil fumbled with the key in the door, her

hands shaking, the sweat pouring off her sickly face. Debbie lunged at the door, but Auntie Lil had locked it and was already at the window, one hand struggling with the catch and the other holding the key high above her head. Debbie rushed at her, kicking at her shins, hitting and scratching in her turn, but Auntie Lil seemed to be oblivious of every assault.

Surely, thought Debbie, it was time someone came home. It was getting dark, surely the others would be back from school soon, or Mum with the babies, or even one of the neighbours would come back from work and come and see what all the noise was about. Then the top sash of the window rattled down beside the lower one — and the door key flew through the opening into the cold, empty street.

Oh please, thought Debbie, please someone come home soon and help me. Please don't let the others get kept in today, or Mum get caught in the rush hour. Auntie Lil climbed onto the windowsill, burbling about spiders and maggots and cockroaches. Debbie tried to pull at her ankles but Auntie Lil trod on her fingers and shouted, "I'll kill you, you big hairy monster, you won't get me, I'm bigger'n what you are and I'll get away through that hole, so I will!"

She had one leg out of the window before Debbie saw what was her intent.

"No!" screamed Debbie, seizing a chair and climbing up beside her. "You'll kill yerself! Stop it, I tells you, you'll break yer neck if you climbs out there!" She leaned out into the icy dusk and called for all she was worth, "Help! Help me, someone — help! Help!"

Mum shepherded her two youngest children wearily through the swing doors, round again at Stephen's insis-

105

tence, and out into Oxford Street.

"Ice cream! Ice cream!" they chanted in unison.

"No, c'mon now," said Mum. "I didn't know it was so late. I didn't think we'd 'ave to spend so long queuing, look."

There were tears and protests that she had promised. Mum was adamant. "C'mon, you two, now. I shan't take you again, see, if you go on like this. Look, there's our bus coming, and I don't want to be too late tonight, with our Deb at home an' all. You can have ice cream another time — besides, it's too cold for that today, innit?"

Two pairs of toes dug into the pavement and passers-by began to turn towards the screams. The queue at the bus stop stretched six deep to infinity.

"Oh come on then," said Mum, seeing a cafe right beside where they were standing. "Have to be a quick one, mind, whatever comes and no arguing. Oh blimey! They're queuing nearly back to Marble Arch in 'ere too." She looked doubtfully at the children, whose mouths had once more begun to open. Then her eyes followed a waitress carrying a large pot of tea. "Oh all right then. In for a penny, in for a pound. They'll just 'ave to manage for theirselves for once, 'cos we ain't 'arf gonna be late back tonight."

Debbie pulled with all her strength, and suddenly, with a crash of breaking glass as Auntie Lil's knee went through the window, they overbalanced together and fell rolling on the bedroom floor. Surely, thought Debbie, someone heard that and would come and see what was the matter — they'd be here soon enough if you didn't want them to hear. Wouldn't Mum *ever* get home?

In a trice Auntie Lil was up at the window again, with

Debbie after her. Debbie opened her mouth to shout for help — and Auntie Lil reached out and caught her by the throat.

"I got you now," she squealed exultantly, "and I'm bigger'n what you are now, ain't I? D'you know what I'm gonna do, then, eh? I'm gonna lock you in that little dark cupboard with all them spiders and wigglies, and you can scream and scream and scream till you're sick!"

Very slowly she began to hoist Debbie up the broken window pane towards the great gaping opening above it.

Marilyn stamped her feet and pouted. It was too bad of that Kevin. First she had waited outside school until everyone had gone and then she had walked to the bombed site and waited another half hour in the perishing cold. And still there was no sign of him. Now it was quite dark and Mum would be furious with her whatever happened. Well, she wouldn't wait any longer: he had probably gone on home by himself long ago. She'd go back and tell Mum he'd given her the slip and if he got into trouble it was his own fault. In Marilyn's opinion he was quite old enough to look after himself anyhow, and not keep his sisters hanging about to escort him everywhere.

There was one thing: when she did catch up with him he wouldn't half cop it for keeping her out so late, and that was a promise.

Debbie's head stuck out of the window while the rest of her struggled to keep a foothold on the windowsill. Suddenly Auntie Lil relaxed the grip on her throat to grasp her lower down, and in the same instant Debbie saw a dim figure standing with upturned face in the road below.

107

"Help!" shouted Debbie. "Oh, help!"

"Whatever is the matter, my dear child?" a familiar voice called back. "Is the house on fire or something?"

"It's me auntie!" called Debbie. "Get someone! Do something — quick!"

Auntie Lil let go of her abruptly and gripped the top of the window frame. Then she leaned out and shouted just two words into the street below.

The angel looked as astonished as if Balaam's donkey had charged him with bared teeth.

TWELVE

As soon as Marilyn left the bombed site and started towards home a fire engine passed her, lights flashing, siren wailing. She stopped to gaze open-mouthed at such splendour at close quarters, but it had gone before she had even finished thinking that she would tell Kevin what he'd missed and serve him right too. Just her luck, she thought, that it didn't stop and put out a fire right there beside her. She had just noticed that the fire engine took the same turning as she would presently take, when a police car raced past in the same direction. Marilyn quickened her pace: the fire might yet be on her route home.

There was no sign of any excitement when she rounded the corner, but she could still hear sirens and bells, so she hurried on, looking hopefully down each side road she passed. Everything was as usual; there was no smell of smoke nor sign of leaping flames, and after all, thought Marilyn regretfully, you could hear a fire engine from many miles away.

She had almost forgotten the whole incident by the time she reached her own street, until she caught sight of flashing lights more or less opposite the very house in which she lived. Marilyn ran the last few hundred yards. It was too bad — the one day there was a fire next door she had to be late back because of that wretched Kevin, and Debbie had been at home all day and wouldn't have missed a minute of the fun.

Then she stopped. A little knot of people stood in the

road gazing up at the windows of the top flat. Their flat. The street door stood open, admitting a traffic of uniformed people. Marilyn suddenly felt quite differently about fire engines.

"What's 'appened?" she demanded, in a voice she didn't recognise.

"Dunno dear," said a woman with a bulging shopping bag. "We was just going home, see."

"Don't think it's a fire at all," said a man. "More like someone took ill or summink. There was an ambulance here a while back."

"Never mind, dear," said another woman to her little boy. "See a fire another day, eh?"

Marilyn started frantically to push her way through them. At the bottom of the steps she was stopped by a policeman.

"Now look here, miss," he said, "I've already asked everyone to keep back. Why don't you go home like a good girl? There's no more to see here."

"Well I'm trying to go home, ain't I?" said Marilyn indignantly. "I lives here, don't I?"

"What's your name, love?"

Marilyn was just about to tell him when a voice above her head called out, "Lyn! Hey, Lyn, Lyn!"

She looked up to see Gloria from below leaning out of the windows.

"'Ere, what's going on?" shouted Marilyn.

"Your auntie got took away to the loony bin, and she locked the door so they had to get her down wiv ladders and she tried to push Deb out the window but Deb shouted for help, and they carried yer auntie down screamin' into the road summink about spiders being after her, and they had to bust the door down and the

110

fuzz come and your mum gets back and starts screamin', and them littl'uns 'owling their 'eads off, and your dad hollering how he knew that there auntie of yours'd do her nut one of these days — "

Gloria disappeared from view suddenly and the window dropped with a thud.

Marilyn didn't wait for any further accounts. She ran up the steps two at a time into the house, and this time no one barred her way.

Debbie was crying. It was a rare event normally reserved for extremes of pain or injustice. She had, mercifully, just been spared both of these, but for some reason the tears still poured down her face and each breath caught in her throat. She sat in the kitchen sipping a mug of scalding tea with three lumps of sugar: the ultimate in having achieved the dizzy leap from fallen grace to the status of Mum's favourite child.

Out of the corner of one swollen eye Debbie watched two policemen at work. One emptied each drawer and cupboard in the kitchen and then slowly and carefully replaced each object as it had been. The other was across the passage apparently doing the same thing in what had recently been Auntie Lil's room. The policemen were not getting tea or any such sign of Mum's favour; not only were they prying into places that were none of their business and adding to the grime on the floor with their boots, but every time Stephen and Carole saw their uniforms they clung to Mum, screaming.

It was cold in the flat. Dad had on his jacket in mute protest against the front door being wide open, admitting not only sundry officials, neighbours and his own family, but a freezing draught from the street below. He was drinking his tea and munching suet pudding doggedly, his

111

thin face giving nothing away to the police sergeant who was asking him questions.

"So you and your wife were both out at the time, Mr Williamson?"

"S'right," said Dad, reaching for the teapot.

"So you don't know if your sister-in-law could have taken anything to cause this — er — brainstorm?"

"Bah! She was always taking things," said Dad. "Never wivout 'em as far as I could see."

"Oh? What sort of things?"

"Sleeping tablets, pills for this, pills for that — you name it, she swallowed it. Proper old maid for tablets, she was. Proper old maid, come to that."

"I see." The sergeant looked up as the two constables approached him with a trayful of oddments, all of which had clearly originated in a chemist's shop. Debbie recognised the cough mixture she had been taking and Auntie Lil's much diminished bottle of sleeping pills. The sergeant sorted through them, handing back all that Mum and Dad vouched for, plus the brand names in Auntie Lil's collection. He was left with a dubious assortment of unnamed medicines, out of date prescriptions and one or two bottles with illegible labels.

"You ought to keep these kind of things in a safer place," he said severely to Dad. "You got young kids and all, look."

Dad jerked his thumb towards Mum and muttered something about her and her sister; he never needed nothink like that, and Mum tried to pretend she hadn't heard and began clearing plates away with a heightened colour.

"I'm going to take these for analysis," said the sergeant, "but I shouldn't think you've got anything to worry about."

Dad gave a short laugh. "It ain't me what's worried, mate," he said.

"Mr Williamson," said the police sergeant, "I don't think you quite understand the position. It is more than likely that your wife's sister is suffering from the effects of taking an hallucinatory drug — probably LSD, which is such a highly dangerous substance that it is illegal in this country. Do you realise that if any of this drug is found on your premises, you, as the tenant, could be held responsible?"

Debbie had stopped crying to hear what the police sergeant was saying, which was just as well because Mum had started to sniff now. Dad was just telling everyone his opinion of Auntie Lil when a policewoman walked into the kitchen. The sergeant got to his feet and explained that she had come to have a little chat with Debbie, whereupon Dad protested loudly that his girls had been brought up nice and didn't know nothing about drugs nor nothing like that, because if he'd ever seen them taking anything, no, he told a lie, if he'd so much as heard them talk about it, he'd have flayed them alive, so help him he would, because you have to be cruel to be kind sometimes and he wasn't having no filthy talk of that sort in his house, he wasn't.

The police sergeant looked mildly surprised and pointed out that as Debbie had been alone with Auntie Lil she might be able to throw some light on what had happened, adding under his breath that their women constables were very experienced and often a child would talk more freely to them than her parents. Dad said that if the Law was going to twist his kid's arm they could twist it right there with him present so he could hear what was said.

Debbie, who felt that anybody's company would be

better than her parents' at that moment, allowed herself to be led into her bedroom by the policewoman while Dad and the sergeant were still remonstrating with each other against a background of Mum's sniffs.

To begin with the policewoman chatted of this and that, asking about school, the holidays and Debbie's expectations for Christmas. Debbie, wary of being drawn, answered with a nod or a monosyllable, watching every move.

"I like your pictures," said the policewoman, indicating the life-size posters of pop stars the girls had stuck on the walls. "Is he your favourite?"

"No," said Debbie.

"Nor mine," said the policewoman, predictably. "Who sleeps in that bed?"

"Kevin," said Debbie. At the back of her mind she felt there was a question she herself wanted to ask, but when the policewoman spoke again it went clean out her head.

"Does Lyn have any boyfriends?"

"What, our Lyn?" said Debbie. "You gotta be joking! Ain't you seen her yet? Cor! *You'd* be more likely to get a feller'n what she is!"

The policewoman seemed so tickled by this compliment that Debbie made a mental note to deflate her when she got the chance. Meanwhile she found herself talking about Terry and Cheryl and even Karen.

"Do they come here often?" the policewoman wanted to know. Debbie disillusioned her completely.

Presently the conversation turned to Auntie Lil and the day's excitement. Yes, her aunt had complained of a headache after dinner. She had threatened to take two of her tablets, the ones in the big bottle the fuzz had pinched, and lie down. No, Debbie had not seen her take

114

them, but those were the ones she took for headaches; Debbie had seen her take them on other occasions, well, she'd talked about them enough times, hadn't she? The next thing Debbie had known was this noise like a dog whimpering. Blow by blow Debbie parted with the whole story. No, she had never seen her aunt like that before. Yes, she had been scared an' all — dead scared. Debbie was getting bored.

"She did say one thing you might want to know," she told the policewoman confidentially.

"When, dear?"

"After dinner, just before Mum went off wiv the littl'uns."

"Yes?" The policewoman leaned just a fraction forward and smiled encouragingly. "Do tell me what she said."

Debbie lowered her eyes demurely and folded her hands in her lap. Then she opened her mouth and let loose a barrage of language that would have made Dad faint. The policewoman drew in her breath sharply. The interview was over.

It seemed quiet in the flat when the police had all gone and the front door was shut.

"Bed time," said Mum. "I'm all in. Come on now, you kids." She took hold of Stephen and Carole and herded them from the kitchen. "Don't take long now, you three," she said to Marilyn. "I don't want to hear no more through that wall."

You three.

Debbie suddenly remembered the question that had come to her mind earlier and had remained unasked.

"Where's Kev?" she said.

THIRTEEN

Mum let go of the little ones and put her hands on her hips. "Well?" she demanded sternly. "Where is he then?"

There was silence. Everyone looked at Debbie.

"Well I dunno, do I?" she said. "That's why I arsted."

"Kevin!" roared Mum. "Come on, out of it! Bed time!"

But there was no answer, and a brief search of all possible hiding places revealed nobody.

"Little varmint," said Dad. "Must've got out while the door was open. What's he think he's playing at?"

"I never see him at all tonight," said Debbie.

"He were here tea time," said Mum, looking frightened. "He were definitely here tea time."

"I never seen him," Debbie insisted. "You sure you see him, Mum?"

"Course I seen him! I knows me own child, don't I? Don't be daft. I sees Marilyn come in and I thinks to meself that's them back from school anyways."

Marilyn looked bewildered. "I never — I mean — he din't come back wiv me — "

"Why not?" Mum turned upon her savagely. "*Why* din't he come back wiv you, eh? You knows what I've told you — you got to come home together. *Now* look what you've done!"

Marilyn's face puckered. "It weren't my fault, Mum! I did wait for him — I waited ages, I did honest; I waited till everyone gone home before I give up, and it were ever so cold, too, but he never come out and I thought he gone home by hisself."

"Course," said Dad, "you never thought to say nothink when you found he ain't here, did you?"

"I — I never thought — " stammered Marilyn. "I saw that fire engine and all them coppers an' all, and I forgot — "

"It ain't Lyn's fault, Mum," said Debbie. "No one noticed he ain't here, look."

"He won't 'arf get noticed when he do come in," said Dad.

"Yeah, but where is he?" said Mum.

Dad gave a kind of snarl. "He'll be off somewheres wiv some of his mates. Terry used to be the same, remember? Nine or ten o'clock at night it were sometimes. Frightened you to death the first time."

"Terry was older," said Mum. "Terry never started stopping out late till he were at the big school, look. Our Kevin's only little."

"Kids grow up quicker these days," said Dad. "Besides, he got the others to copy, ain't he?" He looked pointedly at Debbie.

Mum shifted uneasily from one foot to the other. "Best get these two to bed," she said. "P'raps he'll be back by that time."

But he wasn't.

Debbie and Marilyn undressed without a word and got into bed. Debbie reached up and turned out the light. Somehow it was easier to listen in the dark. Through the slightly-open door she could see that the kitchen light was on, and hear the murmur of voices, though she could only catch occasional words. Mum said something about kids and school, and then she caught the word "police". Evidently Dad didn't like this — Debbie knew that tone of voice well, but all she really heard was: "Dead beat as it is."

117

"Deb — Deb!" Marilyn was whispering.

"Uh?"

"Deb — what d'you think's happened to him?"

"He's OK." Debbie spoke with much more conviction than she felt.

"He weren't round at the bomb site neither," said Marilyn. "I waited hours round there too."

"He'll be back soon," said Debbie. She felt exhausted suddenly and her throat was hurting again. A hundred and one things could have happened to Kevin, and most of them were unthinkable. Soon a rhythmic snoring beside her announced that Marilyn was asleep. There were no more voices from the kitchen. Debbie pulled the bedclothes up over her head, shivering a little, though she wasn't really cold. Presently she too slipped into an uneasy doze filled with Auntie Lil's screams, the fire engine's siren and her own voice trying to shout for help, while all the sound she could make was a rough, rasping whisper nobody could hear.

She jerked awake suddenly, utterly convinced that Kevin's voice had woken her, and, jumping up, she ran into the kitchen, excitedly calling his name.

Dad spun round, staggering, his mouth open, staring in alarm; Mum, a blanket wrapped around her, sat upright slowly, yawning, her eyes dark-rimmed and heavy. Debbie stopped, dazzled in the glare of the electric light. There were only the two of them — no Kevin after all.

"Mum! Mum — I thought — " The words trembled and disintegrated and the next moment Debbie was swept sobbing onto Mum's ample lap.

"Ah, bless her, she's half asleep still, look. Did you have bad dreams, pet — was that it? She's bin 'aving nightmares, and small wonder after what she bin through today and that cold an' all."

She rocked Debbie to and fro as if she had been Carole, stroking her hair as she did so. Presently she spoke again, the sharp anxiety in her voice penetrating this comfortable warmth.

"Just look at the time, Les! It's a quarter to four. We got to do summink soon — I don't care what you nor anyone else says."

"Give it till four then," Dad counselled.

When Debbie woke again she was back in bed and the December substitute for daylight showed in the window. Kevin, she thought instantly, and sat up to look at the bed in the corner. It was flat, cold and empty.

Dad took the girls to school that morning. He said he had to pass the door on his way to the police station, but Debbie, who knew more geography than that, suspected that he wasn't going to risk more than one child disappearing at a time. Ironically, she had been longing to get to school to boast to the others how she had coped single-handed when her auntie had gone stark, staring, raving bonkers and had had to be rescued dramatically by the fire brigade, but now that she was on her way she would have given much to have stayed at home and avoid being questioned about Kevin.

Dad gripped their hands and marched them at double time so that they had to jog to keep up. He had, thought Debbie, his destination written all over him, and his daughters might have been dangerous criminals in custody. As they passed the bombed site he skidded on some frozen slush and almost sat down in the gutter.

"Blimey," he accused them, "how much further to your school?"

Marilyn pointed out that there was no need to run, they were going to be ever so early as it was, and Dad

119

boxed her ears and strode on faster than ever. When they arrived the doors were not yet unlocked and they had to stand in a biting wind, as grim-faced and silent a trio as one could expect to meet within a week of Christmas.

At the end of Assembly Debbie became aware of a stir at the back of the room. There was some whispering she couldn't hear and several pairs of eyes were directed towards the door. She followed their gaze with her own and could just make out something dark outside with bright patches on it. She recognised the effect immediately: polished buttons on a navy blue uniform. Debbie and Marilyn exchanged glances and buried themselves in their hymn books as primly as any Victorian governesses.

When the final prayer had been said, one of the staff stepped up to the front and whispered to the headmaster. He frowned, looked up and caught Debbie's eye for a moment. Then he told everyone to wait in their places and left the room. His return brought complete silence to the gathering: with him walked two policemen and a policewoman.

"Will you all sit down please," said the headmaster.

Briefly, he told them that Kevin was lost and the police were trying to find him. The children were to answer any questions they were asked and were not to be afraid to come forward with anything they had heard or seen which might help, however slight it seemed. The headmaster turned to Mr Webster.

"Kevin's still in your class, I believe. Was he in school yesterday?"

"Yes, he was one of the children who came on the expedition to the Science Museum."

One of the policemen asked whether he could have been left behind in the museum.

"I think it extremely doubtful," said the headmaster.

120

"We do this sort of thing fairly often, you know, and it's never happened before."

"I counted heads as we started," said Mr Webster, "and then again as we came away and the numbers tallied all right."

The headmaster said, "Hands up anyone who remembers Kevin being there yesterday."

One or two rather doubtful arms were raised and subsided. When pressed, one girl said she remembered Kevin taking such a long turn looking at something she had missed hers, while one boy said he had sat next to Kevin in the train, but he couldn't remember whether it had been on the way out or back. Mr Webster explained that anyone conspicuous by his absence could easily have been with the other group. He added that all the children had been under very close supervision and he felt confident that nothing like that could have gone wrong. The headmaster supported him and the policeman said yes, he was sure this was so, but of course he had to check everything.

Throughout the day the police talked to anyone who had anything to do with Kevin. If, as seemed certain now, he had returned with the others after the expedition, then he must have vanished somewhere between school and home. No one had actually seen him leave, though several people remembered Marilyn waiting for him at the entrance. No one confessed to having gone off with him somewhere for a lark after school, despite police assurance that information of this sort would incur nothing but praise for once.

Debbie and Marilyn were called into the library together to answer questions from a large, soft-voiced policeman. He wanted to know if they had any idea, however unlikely, where Kevin could be. Was there a

121

favourite granny or uncle he could have gone to see, or any place like the seaside or somewhere he had ever talked of revisiting? But they shook their heads and looked as blank as they felt. Was there, the policeman wondered, anywhere Kevin would be likely to go and play without telling anyone? Perhaps somewhere he was not supposed to go? They glanced at each other — the merest raising of eyebrows — and shook their heads again. The bombed site had too many implications, and the present amnesty with the police could not be expected to last for ever. And, thought Debbie, with the way in boarded up, Kevin couldn't have got into the houses anyhow.

The policeman watched their faces thoughtfully. Suddenly he smiled and stood up as if the interview were over.

"I expect you've been enjoying the snow, haven't you?" he said. "My kids are just about your age and they've really been making the most of it. We don't get it like this every year, do we?"

They smiled back. "Wish we did," said Debbie.

"You like it, eh?"

"Smashing," said Marilyn.

"Was that your snowman?" said the policeman. "That really super one in the empty square near your home?"

"No," said Debbie quickly, offended that he should think they could be caught as easily as that.

"Ah," said the policeman, "I didn't really think so. Girls don't usually go for the big ones. I mean, it's hard for one thing — girls don't have the patience. I guessed it must've been the boys made that."

"No they never!" Marilyn exploded. "It was girls done all of that! Them boys just ran about throwing snowballs — that's all they did to help!"

122

*

Mum came to fetch them from school, Stephen and
Carole in tow, grizzling about turning out in the cold.
They walked home in silence, carrying paper and tinsel
decorations in numb fingers, for the next day was the
last day of term. The lady from the Welfare was standing
on the doorstep, waiting for them.

"Hullo, Mrs Williamson," she said. "I guessed you
wouldn't be long. Can I come up for a minute? I've been
in touch with the hospital and I've got news of your
sister." She added under her breath, "Sorry about your
other trouble."

Mum heaved the push chair into the dark little hall,
her mouth working. She hoisted Carole in one arm and
began dragging Stephen upstairs with the other. "I don't
know when I went through such a time, I don't really,"
she said.

The Welfare lady helped the little ones with their
coats while Mum made tea. Debbie and Marilyn could
hear most of what she said as they laid the table.

"Your sister's her normal self again, but she's still
very weak and shaken, of course. They think it's almost
certainly LSD — everything would point to that — but
they can't make out how she came by it yet. There was
nothing unusual in any of the bottles they tested, and
she says she didn't have anything the rest of you didn't
have, and nothing outside of this flat."

So, thought Debbie, either Auntie Lil didn't realise it
was the sweet that had done the damage, or she would
not admit to having pinched it. Either way it saved a lot
of awkward explanations and she was grateful to Auntie
Lil for keeping her mouth shut.

"How long'll they keep her in for?" said Mum, dully.

123

"Well — a little while yet, I'm afraid. You see, the — er — nightmares could come back and cause her to do something dangerous again."

Mum said, "You mean, she still might take some more of that stuff?"

"No, no, I'm sure she didn't take it on purpose, and I'm sure she wouldn't take it again for anything after what she's been through, but you see, the effects can come back sometimes long after taking the drug. So you see it wouldn't be safe to send her home too soon, especially with the children."

Mum sat down hard. "But you said — you said she were back to normal — "

The Welfare lady pulled up a chair and spoke so quietly Debbie could hardly hear.

"Yes, the nightmares have worn off now, which is normal after twenty-four hours, and your sister was able to talk about what had happened. But of course it's early days yet to know how much damage has been done."

Mum didn't seem able to grasp what she heard. "What's gonna happen to her then? I mean, they don't keep 'em in 'ospital long, do they, specially not over Christmas. I mean, they ain't got the beds, 'ave they? So where'll she go then, if she ain't right by Christmas?"

The Welfare lady hesitated. "Don't worry, dear," she said. "I'm afraid she'll be in over Christmas. They've got to keep her in for a bit under observation, and to take certain tests."

"Tests? What sort of tests?"

Again the sinister pause and the careful choice of words.

"Tests to see — how well she's got over this. As I told you, there could be damage."

124

"Damage? What to?"

"Mrs Williamson, LSD can be a killer. Your sister has been very lucky really. They've got to find out how lucky. But if it has affected her — her mind, it would be too great a risk to send her back here."

"Then where'll she go? She ain't got nowhere else."

"Let's meet that one when it comes, shall we? But you can be quite certain we'll do our best to get her in somewhere nice and not too far for you to visit."

"A home, d'you mean?" Mum whispered.

"There are homes and homes, dear," said the Welfare lady.

"Our Lil — in a home, at her age! Our Lil — and they'd all know. Oh poor, poor Lil! Whatever is she gonna do?"

Debbie remembered Kevin begging Auntie Lil not to go away, so that he wouldn't be put in her room to sleep. In spite of all her protestations Auntie Lil had gone away and left her room empty — but Kevin wasn't there to worry: he had gone away and left his bed empty too.

FOURTEEN

The weekend became a blur of visits from the police and representatives of different authorities, intermingled with neighbours milling in and out, some to offer help, some to snoop, and some, Debbie suspected, just to gawp. It was a weekend of whispering and weeping, of thick raw mist outside and of confused, unanswerable questions indoors making one feel just as cold in the pit of the stomach.

The press reporters arrived. They wore shabby raincoats permeated with stale cigarette smoke and they jostled their way through the flat in the tracks of the police.

"Is it true, Mrs Williams," they wanted to know, "that you quarrelled with your sister-in-law the day she took LSD?"

"Did you say your son Keith was five or nine?"

"Mrs Wilkinson, may I quote you as saying that Ken has run away from home once before because of trouble over drugs?"

Meanwhile the police cordoned off the bombed site and assured the Williamsons that every possible entrance to the houses had been checked and double checked. Kevin could not possibly be in there: a thorough search had been made of the two places where a child might just have squeezed in, but neither had revealed any marks of invasion, nor was anything to be found beyond them. Debbie was torn between bitter disappointment and relief from a nagging fear of Kevin being found lying in

126

a heap at the bottom of one of those broken basement staircases.

Then the false hopes started. A boy answering to Kevin's description had been seen thumbing a lift on the A1, getting off a bus in Liverpool, breaking into an empty shop near Bristol. . . . Two boys of about the same age were seen in suspicious circumstances on the edge of the canal near Kevin's home: the canal was dragged and the story made the national newspapers.

By Sunday Debbie could bear it no longer. After dinner was cleared away she whispered to Marilyn, "I'm going out for a bit. If they misses me, I gone for a walk but I won't be late."

"I'm coming too," said Marilyn.

Debbie was ready for this. "OK," she said. "I'm gonna run right round the Serpentine. Come on!"

"I ain't gonna do that!" said Marilyn.

Debbie shrugged her shoulders. "See you teatime then." She was gone before her bluff could be called.

Half an hour later she got off the train at Kilburn and walked briskly along Birkenhead Terrace. Someone had left the doormat wedged in the street door of number 215, so she went straight upstairs to Cheryl's room. She knocked but there was no reply. She knocked again, a little harder, and called quietly, "You there, Cheryl? It's me, Deb."

There were footsteps inside and Cheryl opened the door.

"Oh blimey, not you lot again. Thought you was s'posed to be coming to baby-sit. Fat lot of good coming today – I got nowheres to go on a Sunday."

"We only just broke up," said Debbie. She went in and peeped into the cot, whose occupant was for once asleep.

"Don't wake her," said Cheryl automatically. She glanced over Debbie's shoulder as she shut the door behind her. "Where's the rest of 'em?"

"Lyn's at home. She dunno I'm here." She paused and swallowed. "Our Kev's missing."

"What d'you mean, missing?"

"Lost. He never come back from school Wednesday. We dunno where he is. The police an' all's looking for him. I thought p'raps — I din't know whether he might've come here." The idea which had looked so hopeful at lunchtime seemed ridiculous now that it had failed.

"Come here? What for?"

"I dunno. It was the only place I could think of no one else knew to look in."

"Cor," said Cheryl, "our Kev lost! An' they've no idea? Not even the fuzz?"

Debbie snorted. "They dunno less than what we do. They never stops arstin' us to think of places. It's all in the papers. Ain't you read it? Dad went mad when he first seen it, and them folks downstairs kept coming up to see if we read it."

Cheryl looked stunned. "Cor — our Kev," she said again. Then, "Did Terry meet you?"

"Yeah. Thanks," said Debbie. Had it been only a week ago? It seemed more like six months.

"Did he get that bloke out?" said Cheryl.

Debbie shook her head, watching her sister closely. Cheryl clearly had more to say on the subject: she was biting her nails and staring at the sleeping Karen without seeing anything.

"I went round to Terry's garage again yesterday," Cheryl went on presently. "But he gone. Left. No one don't know where he went. He left sudden one day just like that, they said."

128

"What you want him for?" said Debbie.

Cheryl hesitated. "I lost me job," she said at last. "Cos of her, look." She jerked her head towards the cot. "She never stop crying, and one or two customers complained — specially one old faggot — " Cheryl dug her foot viciously into a rip in the lino floor. "She said I was being crool to her, starving her or summink, and the manageress comes round and says I must leave her at home now she's older — wiv a neighbour or someone — and I goes mad, see, and we has this row in front of everyone, and she sez that's that, then, and gives me me cards, and I tells her what she can do wiv her job."

"But what you want our Terry for?" persisted Debbie.

"I'm just telling you, ain't I?" said Cheryl, crossly. She bit her nails savagely for a moment or two and then said, "I got no money, see. I had me purse nicked a while back, an' I'm behind wiv me rent, and her downstairs sez if I don't pay soon she can 'ave me chucked out. I thought p'raps if Terry got that reward for pulling that bloke out he might lend me summink just to take me over Christmas. There's no one won't take you on this time of year, see, and I has to take her everywhere so's they all knows I got her."

A choking sound from the cot made Debbie glance in that direction. The blanket began to ripple as Karen opened first her eyes and then her mouth.

"'Ere we goes again," said Cheryl wearily, pushing her feet into her slippers and shuffling over to the cot. "You best get 'ome," she told Debbie. "Ain't nothink you can do."

Debbie got up and walked slowly to the door.

"Oh — and Deb — I hopes you finds our Kev OK. Come and tell me, will you?"

Debbie nodded, her hand on the door knob. "Cheryl —

Cheryl, you wouldn't — I mean — why don't you — "

Cheryl had her back to Debbie. She lifted the screaming Karen out of the cot, tossing the words over her
shoulder without looking round.

"If you think I'm coming 'ome you got another think
coming, because I tells you straight, I wouldn't spend
Christmas there if it was the very last place in the world
that'd 'ave me!"

Police cars had become so familiar a sight outside the
Williamson home that the other inmates of the house
scarcely bothered to lean out of the windows and stare
at them any longer. Debbie slipped into the flat under
cover of two policemen and had taken up a position in
the corner of the kitchen before anyone realised she
had been missing for the afternoon. Both Mum and Dad
were on their feet in a moment, their eyes on the
inspector rather than their daughter.

"Is it about our Kevin?" Dad asked.

"No more news at the moment, I'm afraid, Mr
Williamson, though the search still continues, of course.
No, we've come to tell you about your sister-in-law this
time."

Mum and Dad sat down again, disappointment in
every line of their faces, and the policemen, now quite
at home themselves, sat down too, unbidden.

"Mrs Williamson, your sister's had a visitor, and we
wondered whether you knew who he was."

"Our Lil? I dunno who'd go an' see her, I'm sure."

"She said —" the inspector coughed slightly and con-
sulted his notebook — "er — 'Tell Doris me fancy man
has been. I bet she don't know as I had one, and no
more did I till he come'."

Mum shook her head. "Did she say who 'e was?"

130

"No. She said she never thought to ask his name till he'd gone. The hospital's been asked to keep a very close watch on anyone trying to visit her, because we still don't know how she came by the drug. Unfortunately Sister wasn't on duty and no one saw him go into the ward or leave it. The nurse in charge couldn't understand how he'd slipped past her because it wasn't really a time they allow visiting as the patients were resting. Our first thought was that she'd either imagined it or dreamt it — she admits she was half asleep when she saw him standing by her bed."

Dad nodded. "Yeah. She bin seeing things again — that'll be it."

"That's certainly how it would appear," agreed the inspector, "but the strange part is that several other patients saw him, too — reliable women with no reason to say they'd seen someone if they hadn't. He seems to have made a very favourable impression too, with a smile and a friendly word to anyone awake. Then again, no one remembers him at reception or in the lift. It's all a bit of a mystery, but the strangest part is what he said to her, and this is really why we're anxious to trace him."

Everyone in the room was listening intently by now. The inspector spoke very slowly and watched each of their faces in turn.

"He said he had come to tell her that both she and Kevin were going to be all right."

"Bah! She's making it up!" said Dad in disgust. "'Ow could anyone know she gonna be OK if the doctors theirselves don't?"

"'Ow'd 'e know anything about our Kev then?" said Mum.

"Exactly," said the inspector. "How indeed does he know anything about Kevin? And how did he know where

131

to find your sister like that? We've been careful not to give the name of the hospital."

"She's just making it all up," insisted Dad.

"No, I don't think so, Mr Williamson. After all, your sister-in-law doesn't know about Kevin's disappearance herself, so why should she say he'd be all right? No, we think the evidence is too strong; we think she did have a visitor who for reasons best known to himself did not wish to be seen by any of the staff. We think he knows more about you all than you realise yourselves, and, what is more, unless he comes forward soon and explains his very suspicious behaviour to our complete satisfaction, we shall be forced to think that he has had a great deal to do with both dope-pushing and kidnapping."

Mum was hardly listening any more. "He said he were gonna be all right? He did say that, din't he?" she pleaded.

"So I understand from your sister. You cling to that, Mrs Williamson, because I do too. Whoever he is, and whatever he's up to, he means the boy no harm, it seems."

Tears of relief were pouring down Mum's face. The inspector looked away politely and said to Dad, "We've only got one other clue at the moment, and that's taken us nowhere yet. This man, whoever he is, told your sister-in-law it was him who raised the alarm when he saw her up at the window."

"HIM?"

The word came out like a cork from a bottle as Debbie leapt to her feet and confronted the inspector. "You don't mean the old bloke what fetched the fire engine after I screamed blue murder? The one Auntie was ever so rude to?"

"I certainly do. She said she apologised to him when she heard he'd saved her life."

"Then we knows him!" cried Debbie, triumphantly. "Us kids knows him, don't we, Lyn? And that means our Kev *is* OK, 'cos that old bloke's ever so clever, he knows everythink, and he knows how to get in and out of places no one else can, just like he did the 'ospital. And he's ever so nice, ain't he, Lyn?"

The inspector exchanged glances with the constable and held up his hand for silence.

"Stop a minute, Debbie," he said, "there's a good girl."

"Debra!" rapped out Mum, dabbing her eyes ferociously on one of Dad's handkerchiefs.

"Look, let's get this straight," said the inspector. "You and Lyn know this man, but your mum and dad don't; is that right?"

"Yeah," said Debbie. "We seen him often. In Cheryl's caff and selling chestnuts and in — in — in lots of places," she ended lamely.

"Has he ever spoken to you?"

"Course he has! He always speak to us. He's ever so friendly. Last time — not when Auntie Lil done 'er nut, before that — he tell us not to trust no one. That sort of thing. Kind, like."

"Did he indeed? And do you know his name?"

Debbie's brow furrowed. "Don't think he got one. He ain't like other people, see."

"Oh? What makes you say that?"

"He said so, din't he, Lyn?"

"Yeah." Marilyn sniggered. "Said he were a angel," she confided.

"He said what?" The inspector looked sharply from one to the other of them; then he said to Debbie, "Did you hear him say that too?"

"He were only kidding." Debbie's cheeks were crimson. Marilyn had betrayed them all, including the stranger, to open ridicule.

"He weren't!" said Marilyn indignantly. "You believed him too, Debra Williamson. He said as he don't wear feathers no more in case he gets took for a pigeon."

"Sounds like you two been taken for a ride," said the inspector. "Now listen," he added, in such a serious voice that they did. "You two girls aren't babies any more and you want to help us find Kevin, don't you? Good. Now I want you to come and let us know immediately if you see this man again. He may well be able to give us valuable information. Don't – er – don't waste time telling him we're looking for him – best not stop to talk to him at all. Just keep a sharp look out in all the places you've seen him in, and if you do spot him come and tell us *at once*. Do you understand?"

They nodded. Marilyn's eyes were round with awe, but Debbie looked uncomfortably at her feet. The angel had been their friend; she disliked the idea of spying on him. After all, he had been good enough to warn them not to trust anyone, and she knew for a certainty he was not responsible for giving that sweet to Auntie Lil.

"He ain't like that," she told the inspector, stubbornly. "He's good. I knows he is."

"Look here, Debbie," said the inspector, "if your friend's innocent he need have nothing to fear from the police. In fact he'll want to help, won't he? So you can't do any harm putting us in touch with him, eh? But if he's giving you all sorts of warnings against people, he may not be all he seems, in which case the sooner we find out the better. Isn't that so? We can't afford to take any risks with Kevin, now can we?"

"But – what you think he done?"

"I don't know that he's done anything yet, but he sounds a strange fellow and if he's not quite right in the top storey he may need help. He may even have been warning you to keep clear of himself. Very often that sort of person can tell when he's likely to have one of his — er — turns, and he doesn't want to harm you while he's not himself. Does that make sense to you?"

Debbie nodded, too appalled to argue any more. It made very good sense, although she did not wish to believe it was true.

The inspector went on, "Has he ever offered you anything — at the cafe or anywhere? Drinks or sweets or anything like that? Did he promise to bring you anything at any time?"

"Yeah!" The memory came flooding back — surely proving the stranger's innocent intentions. "Yeah! He said he come to bring us Christmas! Not like just the date an' that, but real, proper Christmas!"

"Hm. Sounds as if he'd had a bit too much Christmas himself, if you ask me. Look here — you girls are quite old enough to understand me: your auntie was made very, very ill by taking drugs, wasn't she? Now that particular sort she took can affect different people in lots of different ways. It can make you see things and hear things that aren't there at all. It can make you think you can do things that are impossible, like fly or drive a car straight through a brick wall. Or it can make you think you are someone or something that doesn't exist. Do you get the point of what I'm saying? Now if this poor chap is just a vagrant who's got hold of some of the same stuff as your auntie — well, the sooner we stop him doing any harm to himself or anyone else, the better."

FIFTEEN

Mr Webster looked out of place in the flat, like parents did in school when they came to the concert. He had come to ask whether he might take the girls to the local cinema that afternoon; there was a U programme with a Western as the main feature. He might have been asking for both their hands in marriage, Debbie thought, Mum was acting so suspicious.

"I'll have to arst their dad first," she kept saying.

"I'm afraid it'll all be over by then," said Mr Webster.

"Oh Mum, he's our *teacher*! We'll be OK with him!"

"I dunno . . . It's ever such a responsibility on me own . . . and wiv our Kevin gone — " She broke down, pressing a damp tea towel to her eyes.

"I know how you feel, Mrs Williamson," said Mr Webster. "I just thought it might help to take their minds off things for a few hours — and give you a bit of a break. The strain must be terrible."

"Oh please, Mum, *please*!" they begged.

"I dunno — " Mum was wavering, visibly. "I mean it's not like someone I knows. Their dad wouldn't like them to be going wiv strangers at their age."

"Oh *Mum*!"

To Debbie's relief Mr Webster seemed amused rather than offended. "I wouldn't hear of it either," he agreed, "but I'm hardly a stranger. I see them every day at school, you know."

"Well — " said Mum. "OK then, this once. But don't be late — "

"I'll have them back by six," Mr Webster promised.

To their mortification Mum followed them out of the flat and leant over the banisters watching them all the way down to the hall.

"What she think we gonna do?" whispered Marilyn.

"It's what's *he* gonna do, she's on about," replied Debbie.

It was a good film: the girls sucked sweets and escaped thankfully into a world of thrills and glamour. Coming out into the raw darkness of the London winter made the ache of Kevin's absence bite more deeply than ever.

"You all right, Debbie?" said Mr Webster anxiously, and she nodded, the tears running through her fingers as she pretended to cover her face from the cold.

"We'll get a cup of tea in here before I take you back," he said, herding them into a little place off Praed Street smelling comfortingly of coffee and hot buns. For a while they sipped in silence, then Mr Webster said: "Look — we're all thinking about the same thing, better talk it over than bottle it up, don't you think?"

Unwillingly at first, Debbie found herself going over again each interview with the police, each step of the story from the time she was left alone with Auntie Lil to the moment Kevin's disappearance was discovered.

"You don't think Kevin gave your auntie anything to eat for a lark?" suggested Mr Webster. "Like in her tea or anything, and then got frightened and ran away?"

"He weren't there," said Debbie. "It were only me wiv her."

"And you'd ate — " began Marilyn — "Ouch!" She looked resentfully at Debbie and tucked her feet smartly back out of reach.

"Sorry Lyn," lied Debbie, sweetly. "I'd ate the same dinner as her and all of 'em," she finished quickly.

But Mr Webster didn't seem to have noticed anything suspicious. He sat stirring his tea, frowning deeply.

"There's just one thing that bothers me," he said at last. "The day you were away from school, Debbie, we had some carpentry wood stolen. Kevin was convinced he'd seen it, nailed across one of the doors to those empty houses. I went to have a look this morning but I couldn't see a sign of it. I can't help wondering whether Kevin could have gone there after school to investigate, and got — er — mixed up with something. Look — I know you three used to go and play there sometimes — did you ever notice anything strange or unusual in any way when you were there?"

The tip of Debbie's shoe just brushed Marilyn's shin under the table. Marilyn pouted but the warning was enough. "No," she said, unblinkingly.

"Only this old bloke," said Debbie. "We did wonder 'ow he got in and out."

"What old bloke?" Mr Webster seemed alarmed.

"We tell the fuzz about him, but not we met him there, 'cos we din't want 'em to know we bin in, see."

"D'you mean the man the police want to interview? You saw *him* there, did you? When?"

Debbie shrugged. "Dunno. Week or more now. He's OK. Honest."

Mr Webster was staring at them blankly, looking worried and upset. Presently he said, "Listen Debbie, I don't like it. I wasn't going to tell you, but I think perhaps I should now. I saw him hanging around there myself, this morning. I got the impression he's squatting in one of those houses. I wouldn't mind betting he's up to no good, and what's more, that if anyone knows anything about Kevin, he does. The sooner the police catch up with him the better. But in the meantime you

138

two had better keep well away from there, especially as I'm going away for Christmas tomorrow and can't keep an eye on you. Come on now, it's high time I took you home again."

They walked into the flat as the news came on just before six. And without any warning, there on the screen was Kevin — Kevin in a tee shirt, with an ice cream in his hand. Debbie stared at him, taking in snatches of what the announcer was saying: ". . . still missing from his home in Paddington . . . police wish to interview a man . . . may answer to the name of Angel . . . "

She remembered vividly the day that snapshot had been taken: a Sunday in June when Dad had taken them all to Hampton Court — a day of sunshine and buttercups and the smell of new-mown grass. They had picnicked and played games and gone through the maze. Get lost, thought Debbie. That was the last thing she had ever said to him, and he had gone off to school and done exactly that.

Then the picture was gone; there were strangers on the screen and the greyness of winter had returned, and Kevin seemed suddenly more remote than he had ever been before.

"Mum," said Debbie next morning, "Mum, can I go down and play with Bernadette for a bit after dinner? I'll come straight up again if Mrs Purdie says no."

Mum looked at her for a moment and then nodded absently. Debbie guessed that she had hardly heard the request, and turned her energies from tactics to preparation. She put on an old jersey underneath the one she was wearing, and changed into her school shoes, hiding her slippers in a drawer. Then she removed a small parcel from the back of the same drawer: it had Christmas trees all over it and was labelled *To Kev from Deb*. She looked at it regretfully for a minute or two and then ripped the paper off, stuffing it back in the drawer with the slippers. She put the contents quietly into her coat pocket as she passed the hooks by the front door.

As soon as the meal was over Debbie crept out of the flat, pulling on her coat as she went downstairs. Her timing had been meticulous: permission had been granted long enough ago that Mum would not remember she was on the point of going out; on the other hand if she were missed, the reason would be called to mind before there was panic. Mrs Purdie did not refuse permission either; this was because she was never approached. Debbie went straight on down the stairs, past where Gloria lived, through the spicy haze of cooking on the second floor, and at last, still unseen, out into the street.

There was no one about. Debbie made her way quickly to the bombed site and wriggled under the fence as fast as she could. The snowman was still there — two mounds of hard-packed ice with the semblance of features in the top one. Debbie went carefully, leaving no footprints on the frozen surface, intent upon finding the way in that they had all used before. She recognised it immediately: the boards that could be inched to one side at the bottom, and the window with the jagged panes of glass through which they had all stared with such concentration. Mr Webster had been right: there was no wood barring the way any more.

Debbie looked furtively around, but the place was deserted; no children kicked up the greying, ice-covered rubble, and no dark uniforms showed beyond the mesh gate. She pressed the boards at her feet: they gave as they had done before and she squeezed through into the room beyond.

The boy's thermos and the things they had brought for him were not there; she wondered who had found them, and how long ago. There was no sign, either, of anyone having been in the room since she had last seen it herself. She looked carefully in the corner where they had found the angel, but there was not so much as a crust or a fag end – not even a tell-tale feather in evidence of his existence. Only then did she realise that she had been fully expecting him to be waiting for her as before, and was bitterly disappointed not to find him. She had not, however, gone to all that trouble just to give up now, and set herself to thinking out the problem. Even if the boy had struggled this far and removed the things they had brought him, he still could not have taken out those nails from inside the building. Someone had gone to considerable trouble removing that wood, and whoever it was had not done so just to pinch the things they'd brought for Joe, because those could not be seen from outside. The more she thought about it, especially in the light of what Mr Webster had said, the more she felt sure the angel had returned to the house and she would find him somewhere there.

And, of course, thought Debbie, optimism rising to the surface again, if you had a whole row of houses to choose from, you would look for a room in one of them that did not have a shattered window and a door that shivered in the wind. She set off to explore.

The dim little hall was just as she had seen it last. She opened the doors on each side and peeped in, seeing nothing remarkable in either. As before, the one on the right held that strange, indefinable smell of burning which reminded her of something or someone. . . . It wasn't the angel, though, she was sure, much as she would have liked to persuade herself it was proof of his

141

having been there recently. She didn't open the door down to the basement. While there were other places to look, there was no need to investigate the possibility that Joe had never made it up those stairs.

Debbie decided to try the other floors. She went upstairs with extreme caution; one or two steps were broken or came loose as she trod on them, and one was missing altogether, leaving a black gap beneath it big enough for one's whole foot to slip through.

The first floor was just like the ground in plan, but brighter. She studied the wallpaper with interest: the one on the stairs had stripes with gold medallions between, bleached almost white near the windows and still darkly vivid in squares that the pictures must have covered. In one room only a corner had survived the ravages of damp and vandalism — a tracery of greens and purples with exotic birds perching and swooping between. Debbie gazed, entranced, almost forgetting why she was there, when suddenly her attention was wrenched away by a slight sound somewhere in the house. She went out onto the landing and listened, but everything was so quiet she decided she must have imagined it.

She went into the room opposite and stood for a moment trying to guess how it had looked furnished. The chimney-piece had carving on it which Debbie thought beautiful. She ran her fingers up and down the fluted columns on either side and into the intricacies of the pattern above — and then she stopped because she thought she heard the same sound as before. She tiptoed to the stairs and leaned over as far as she could without putting any weight on the broken banisters.

The daylight was just beginning to fail. Debbie could see nothing below her, and in any case was not absolutely certain that the sound came from downstairs.

142

"Anyone there?" she called out.

Her voice sounded small, and rang in the emptiness of the house, and there was no reassuring answer from the angel. She went up to the next floor, but this was empty too, just more echoing rooms and a bathroom with the wash basin and all the pipes ripped out, leaving gaping holes in the walls and floor.

Then, and this time unmistakably, the noise came again — a kind of scuffle, followed by a silence that seemed to be waiting for her to make the next move.

Rats, thought Debbie in alarm. Rats, come in to shelter from the cold.

She crept to the top of the stairs and listened anxiously. Was that breathing she could hear, or just the sighing of the wind in the cracks between the boards? She strained her ears while the sound became a measured panting with a rhythmic thud behind it. For a minute or two she listened with increasing panic, then suddenly she realised it was her own heart beat she could hear, and her own frantic breathing.

Debbie bit her lip savagely. "You daft ape!" she said out loud. "It weren't even mice! It weren't nothing but yerself, you silly cow!"

She had reached the top of the house now, and still there was no sign of the angel. She had one foot on the stairs to come down again when the same slow scuffle came again, and this time she distinctly heard a floor board creak far below her.

Debbie stopped. Blimey, she thought, if them's rats, they're big as alsatians!

"'Oo's there?" she called out in a voice that was high and strange in her own ears, and, in the silence that followed, the words that had come to her mind reminded her of the notice on the gate outside. *Guard Dogs . . . .*

There ain't none, she told herself severely. We never seen none — they just writes that to frighten you.

Nevertheless, they had never been into the houses when it was so nearly dark. Besides, there was something down there that didn't answer when you called to it — something that stopped and listened when you moved, something heavy enough to make the floor boards creak beneath its tread.

Debbie began to shiver. She dared not risk going downstairs now for fear of the creature lurking in the shadows, hackles bristling, snarling lips slavering over yellow, pointed fangs. It would be crouching ready to spring on her, she could practically feel its great paws crushing her chest and smell its fetid breath. It would hold her down, growling and snapping at her throat, till the police came to punish her next morning, or maybe — an even more dreadful thought struck her — maybe trespassers were the rightful perk of the dutiful guard dog on its long night watch, and it would tear her in pieces, grinding her bones in its jaws.

Kevin, she thought suddenly. Had he come, all unsuspecting, to be hunted and finally cornered by a wolf-like monster, so that if they found him at all he would be nothing but a little mangled mess of undigested left-overs?

Debbie looked wildly round for a way of escape, her head singing with fear. The only route she could see that did not involve going downstairs was a trap door in the ceiling, presumably leading to the roof and the fire escape beyond. It was hanging half open and looked as if it might be one of those that have an extending step ladder attached. It was quite out of reach and she began to think desperately of something she could stand on to lend her an extra foot or so. Then she remembered the

144

broken wash basin and went as quietly as possible into the bathroom. It was too heavy and noisy to drag out into the passage, but there had been a fitted cupboard round it which was not fixed to the floor and which she was able to carry out and place under the trap door to form a sort of three sided box. From here she could just reach the ring handle above her, and by leaning all her weight upon it she managed to pull most of it down to her level.

It was much warped and partly broken, but she climbed onto the bottom of it eagerly, kicking away the box platform beneath her to discourage the dog from following her lead. Then she scrambled up into the darkness of the attic ahead. Once inside she tried to pull up the steps, but could not reach far enough to make them budge. For a moment she lay still, panting and exhausted, but then she realised that the dog would soon be on her trail, bounding up those steps and sniffing her out in the darkness.

Debbie sat up and looked around her. Straight ahead was a square of sky, presumably the door out onto the roof. As her eyes began to adjust to the dim light she took note of her position. The floor was a network of wooden joists between which there were craters and jagged holes whichever way she looked. Clearly, she must keep to the wooden parts and hope they would take her weight. Very slowly, with trembling knees, she picked her way to the opposite side. Occasionally the rib bent beneath her, and once there was an ominous crack which echoed round the floor like ice that will not bear the skater, but eventually she made the distance across and came within reach of the door with its little grey window.

It was at that moment that she heard something move

145

behind her. She started round in terror, quite expecting to see a great bristling shape lunging towards her through the hatchway, but instead there was a rattle and a slam, and the trap door which Debbie had been unable to pull up, was shut fast by someone on the other side.

SIXTEEN

A dog could not have done it. However far she stretched her imagination, Debbie knew this must be so. Whoever had been following her round the house and had now shut the attic door on her must be a human being, and a full grown one at that.

The next minute she was starting back excitedly towards the way she had entered.

"You silly twit," she scolded herself out loud. "You come 'ere to meet him, ain't you? So why all the carry on when he shows up then, eh? How were he to know it were you up here?"

Then she stopped. She had called out to him — twice. He must have known it was her, and he had not answered. He had just kept quiet and followed her. Perhaps he hadn't heard her, though — perhaps he genuinely hadn't known there was anyone there but himself. . . . But she had heard him quite clearly when he had stepped on the floor board.

Debbie sat down where she was, no longer able to perform the balancing act across the joists of the attic. Whichever way she looked at it, the truth was unavoidable: the strange man who had said he was an angel was in the house; he knew she was there too; he had followed her upstairs without making himself known, and he had deliberately shut her in the attic.

Suddenly it was all too much for her, and Debbie put her hands up to her face, mingling the dust and grime from the house with her frightened and frustrated tears.

Why? Why had he treated her like this when they had been such friends and she had stood up for him so often? What had she done to make him change so suddenly and disastrously towards her? She would have given anything to run home and howl to Mum how mean and unfair he had been — but she was trapped in a dark and dangerous prison, and this time, such was her own ingenuity that no one, not even Marilyn, knew where she was. She crawled miserably back to the trap door, and listened.

"'Ere, Mister!" she pleaded softly, but her voice came out so hollow and husky that it gave her the creeps, and in any case she was not sure she really wanted to be heard.

But what would happen if she did not let anyone know she was there? Presumably she would spend the night on the hard, ribbed floor in the dark, and not only that night but the next day, and Christmas, and the whole holidays too, with nothing to eat, getting weaker and weaker and colder and colder . . . until one day, when the demolition people came to clear the site at last, and their bulldozers and drills ate into the houses one by one along the row, a little bundle of rags would be found at the top of one of them, covering a long-forgotten heap of human bones.

Debbie opened her mouth to scream the place down, but the sound stuck in her throat as the inspector's words came vividly to mind: "Don't stop and talk to him at all." They had all told her the same thing, and because it hadn't suited her to listen, she had stubbornly contradicted them; she had brushed aside their warnings and set off alone to the very place where she knew him to be hiding out — and walked straight into the trap he had set for her without telling anyone else where she was going.

148

What if they had been right about him? The thought, which had begun as a niggle, became a panic. After all, she had no proof of his identity; on the contrary, she had doubted it from the very beginning. He himself had warned them to trust no one; could he really have meant that there were moments when he went out of his mind and could kill? She pictured the gentle, courteous stranger — and then suddenly she thought of poor, silly, harmless Auntie Lil . . . Auntie Lil, who had, without warning, become possessed of superhuman strength, who had locked her in, tearing at her wrists with hands of iron, and who had grabbed her by the neck and pulled her mercilessly towards an open, fourth floor window . . . .

The stranger had witnessed this happen, he had gone to see Auntie Lil, and he had known, somehow, about Kevin. What had he known, she wondered? Could he, by some awful chance, have got hold of one of those same sweets and be suffering from the same terrible madness as Auntie Lil? And if so, for heaven's sake, *what had happened to Kevin*?

"No!" whispered Debbie, hoarsely. "No! Please, no!"

In her imagination she saw the mad stranger coming very slowly up the stairs again, getting nearer and nearer, still smiling — only this time the smile was a sly grin and he licked his lips a little as he came, nodding his head knowingly from side to side as he climbed higher and higher, until at last the trap door dropped open again and he was there in the attic, his eyes staring, his great hands stretched out towards her, and on them would be a pair of thick, black, blood-stained gloves.

Debbie started up and began to stumble towards the door to the fire escape. Several times she slipped, scraping her ankles against the rough ribs of wood, and once her foot broke through the rotten covering of lath and plaster, making the dust rise in a suffocating cloud around her. When she reached the door again she hardly had the strength to grasp the handle, so that it seemed nothing short of a miracle when it opened easily and she stepped outside onto the roof.

For a moment she stood there, leaning against the little brick parapet, drinking in the outside air in deep, reassuring swallows. She could not rest for long though, for the mad stranger might appear behind her at any moment. She began to wonder which way to go next. If she turned right there was no way down outside; the fire escape was at the other end of the row. But along to the left was the avalanche of tiles she and Terry had met before. There was one other house between herself and this block in her escape route, and the attic door to this one had been broken off its hinges altogether. She dared not risk climbing the pile of tiles in the half light with no Terry to hold onto, so she went into the next door house and looked around.

This attic had clearly been converted into an extra room at some time: there was a floor over the wooden joists and instead of a folding step ladder Debbie was relieved to find a short, steep stairway. She went down it, peering from right to left in the shadows for somewhere to hide should she hear footsteps overhead.

It was much darker in this house, the boards on the windows shutting out most of what was left of the daylight. Debbie made her way cautiously towards the stairs, her hands out sideways, touching the walls as she went. Her foot felt the first descent, and there she stopped, remembering the miserable state of the staircase in the next door house. She put her hand into her pocket; it was time to make use of a piece of equipment

150

she had brought with her and almost forgotten.

The torch's thin yellow beam made the surrounding darkness complete. When she directed it at the stairs she could just see where she was treading — and nothing else at all. Debbie inched her way down very slowly, still holding the wall with one hand. Apart from the attic this house was in a much worse state of repair than the other. There was no elegant wallpaper here witnessing to more gracious days: Debbie clung to rough plaster full of holes and open cracks. It smelt of mould and felt damp to her hand.

The first floor landing bent and squeaked beneath her, and much of the woodwork had rotted away altogether. At each creak of her own tread Debbie glanced anxiously upwards, listening, but there was no sign of her pursuer. At the top of the last flight she came to a barrier of two stout wooden bars nailed across in a forbidding X, and on these NO ENTRY was written, unequivocally, in letters of red paint.

Debbie shone the torch through them down the stairs. It was not difficult to see the reason for the warning. A little lower, where the flight took a U turn, there were no steps to be seen at all — just an untidy heap of rubble like a mountain path that has weathered away. The beam of light just reached the bottom of the staircase, where it picked out faintly a similar barricade at ground level.

Debbie considered. To go up again, perhaps into the arms of a murderous maniac, was unthinkable. The only alternative was to risk the descent ahead and hope to find some way out of the house before he caught up with her. As she squirmed through the barrier the torch gave a little warning flicker and dimmed noticeably. The battery, never very strong, Debbie suspected, was rapidly beginning to fail.

151

At the bend in the stairs she stopped. From close to, the pile of debris she had to surmount looked even more dangerous. Worse still, the dim light from the torch now revealed what looked like a gaping hole in the middle, which had not been visible from above. It was impossible to see how deep this pit was, but presumably it went down to street level at least, and possibly even further, through the ground floor and into the basement. That was a long way to fall, particularly if you did so with a broken stone staircase on top of you.

Debbie was about to turn round and go up again when she heard something above her. It was a faint click like turning on a light switch. She put the torch out and sat down to listen, instantly imagining all sorts of noises round her in the darkness. That tapping for instance: it could be a tree against a window, or mice — or floor boards contracting in the colder night air. Then again it might be none of these, but a man moving ever so quietly and stealthily nearer and nearer to where he had seen that tiny point of light.

Debbie switched on the torch and shone it wildly round overhead, but the frail beam showed nothing beyond the barrier through which she had just come. It struck her suddenly that if she found the staircase daunting, how much more so would it seem to a full grown man. If she could once get past the worst part of the flight, then if he followed her at all his weight might easily be too great for what remained of the stairs.

This of course was always supposing her own would not bring about a collapse first. At any rate she felt less afraid of the cold, inanimate chasm ahead than of the warm, gloved hands of the maniac creeping up and reaching for her throat.

Her mind made up, she stood up and switched on the

torch again. Nervously, she edged forward into the loose chippings on the next few steps. So far, so good: there was still a firm base beneath her. Then suddenly there was no step on which to tread — her foot went on going down. Terrified, she jerked it up, clutching at the banisters, her weight still on the other leg to hold her back. She felt around gingerly with her toe, and presently found a firm platform to one side of her. It appeared to be of wood, like a scaffolding plank, and with some relief she risked both feet upon it and began to edge her way through the rubble. Some of the debris she dislodged rattled into the hole; it seemed a long time before she heard it arrive at the bottom, like dropping a stone into a well.

And then, without any warning, the plank sagged beneath her with a tearing, splitting noise, quite deafening in the darkness. Debbie gave a frightened little shriek and leaped as far as she could towards the bottom of the stairs. For a moment she thought she had reached safety, and then the ground under her began to slip sideways as if shaken by an earthquake. She scrambled wildly with her legs amongst the moving rubble, and just as she could struggle no longer, there was solid stone beneath her and she was running down the last few stairs towards the bottom barricade.

On the other side of it she turned to see what was happening to the staircase. At that moment the wall she had been leaning against not two minutes earlier collapsed in a thundering ruin of bricks and plaster just across the hall from where she stood.

Debbie covered her head with her arms and cowered until the noise had stopped. Then she got up, spitting grit out of her mouth and wiping the dust from her eyes. She shone the torch overhead to inspect the damage,

153

looking up into a black dome of nothingness. The staircase no longer existed; there was just a great open mouth in which the jagged edge of the first floor landing grinned like a row of broken teeth above her. She stood among heaps of crumbling brickwork and rotten timber, reaching beyond the scope of the dying torch battery in any direction she looked.

"Don't mind me, will you!" said Debbie out loud in a small, shaky voice. "Hey!" she added. "Pity that barmy old bloke weren't right behind me on them stairs after all!"

There was no question now of returning the way she had come, nor was she willing to explore any further along the row. Her only hope lay in getting back into the next door house and out by her original place of entry. Unfortunately, the wrong wall had collapsed, giving easy access to the house on the further side of the one in which she stood. Debbie was not enthusiastic enough for any more masonry falling about her ears to wish for too easy a way out of this predicament. She studied what was left of the ground floor and realised it was exactly like a looking-glass version of the first house. She went into the room that led to the garden, but there were no loose boards or way out here, so she returned to the hall. The door to the basement staircase was jammed, and she wasn't prepared to risk pulling too hard.

The door on the left presumably corresponded with the room which had the queer bonfire smell in the first house. As she realised this, Debbie remembered something. There had been a small cavity in the wall of that other room which she had suspected led into this very house.

Cautiously, she pulled open the door. It was not properly shut but it stuck on the floor as if warped by

154

the damp, and the handle came off in her hand. She jerked at the door but some bits of plaster dropped on her head, and as the opening was just wide enough to admit her she decided to leave well alone. Debbie flattened herself against the door frame and inched her way through, unable to breathe until the whole of her stood on the other side.

This room had the same smell as its counterpart, and another more familiar one added. She recognised it immediately as joss sticks — someone had brought some to school once and burnt them in the girls' cloakroom at dinner time. Debbie had disliked the smell and had secretly suspected that everyone else had too, though most of them had pretended to enjoy it. There had been sniggers and whispers amongst the older children, and a great scene when Mrs Cowan had discovered them, with all the staff hunting about as if they hoped to find more. Then it had all blown over and that had been the end of the matter.

Debbie turned her attention to the end wall. There was indeed a corresponding gap in it — not a very big one but she reckoned she could just about get through it into the next door house. She put the torch out again to save the last of the battery for the final part of her escape, and began to squeeze through bit by bit, first one arm, then her head — and then she dropped the torch.

Debbie swore softly to herself as she finished squirming through the wall. Then she began to grope about on hands and knees amongst the plaster. She hadn't heard it fall, but between the two rooms was a narrow gap in the masonry, and at the bottom of this she could feel dirt and something soft like rotten wood. She felt about as far as she could reach, supposing the torch must have rolled as it fell. Suddenly she felt something solid and

155

smooth but there was another, and another — a pile of firm, rounded objects lying in the gap in the wall between the two houses.

Much mystified, Debbie continued her search, and presently perseverance was rewarded and she grasped the torch in her hand. She did not immediately make her escape, however; curiosity got the better of her, and she just had to know what she had felt down there. She pressed the button and a flickering, feeble glow revealed for one moment dozens of small, white, polythene-covered parcels.

Then the battery expired and a familiar voice spoke out of the darkness.

"Well, Debbie, so you did decide to come here after all!"

SEVENTEEN

Dad came home that evening to a scene of the utmost depression. The two little ones were grizzling and whining over a toy lorry, flaunting it by turns to perpetuate the quarrel. Marilyn sat with her eyes on the television, her mind as blank as even she could make it. The domestic comedy being shown was drawing to a close: the couple in it were having a monumental row, the hysteria of the studio audience competing with the yells of the comedians and the screams of Stephen and Carole.

Mum, though less noisily, added to the general dejection. She was wandering to and fro between the kettle and the cupboard and the table, putting something out, moving something else, and shuffling back again, and all the time she talked out loud to herself, while the tears trickled unchecked down her swollen face.

"Let's see now — there's jam — kettle ain't boiled yet, no . . . We ain't heard nothink today — they ain't bin near us since . . . Ain't much milk here — oh, sugar, yes — come on kettle . . . I don't think they really knows . . . Get outa me way, you kids . . . They oughter know, it's their job — where is he then, that's what I wants to know . . . Bread — that's empty — where's the new one? I knows I got one — oh me head! Place seems empty without him, poor little soul — he never harmed no one — what they done wiv him then? Sick an' tired of them police, I am . . . There's the bread, look . . . 'Ave I put the tea in?"

Dad switched to another channel when he came in,

saw it was the news and switched off altogether. In the sudden silence the lorry ran under a cupboard and its would-be possessors lost interest immediately.

"Where's our Deb, then?" said Dad. "She ain't surely out again?"

"She gone downstairs to Purdies," Marilyn told him.

"Why ain't you wiv her?" he asked sternly.

Marilyn shrugged. "Bernadette ain't my friend."

"You knows I don't like you girls going out alone," said Dad.

"She ain't gone out," Marilyn insisted. "Only downstairs, like."

"I don't like you going there," said Dad. "That Mrs Purdie ain't too partic'lar in her person, and she don't keep her kids all that, neither. Them littl'uns wets on the stairs. I seen 'em do it."

"Shall I go down and tell Debbie tea's ready?" Marilyn offered.

"You'll do no such thing, my girl," said Dad. "Debra's old enough to know what time it is. If she chooses to miss her tea then she goes to bed 'ungry, and that's all there is to it. I ain't saying a word, look."

"There she is anyway," said Marilyn, as the top door bell rang.

But it wasn't Debbie. It was Cheryl.

She looked round at them all uncertainly and said, "Hullo."

Mum nodded to her, coolly, and turned her full attention to the tea bags.

"'Oo's she, then?" said Dad

"Oh *Dad*!" said Marilyn.

"Well 'ow was I to remember, after she ain't bin near us for so long?" he said.

"Did they find our Kevin yet?" said Cheryl.

158

There was no answer, but Mum wiped her eyes on her apron and sniffed.

"How'd you know about that then?" said Dad.

Cheryl shrugged. "Thought everyone knew."

"Well you ain't only come to arst that," said Dad. "Find you can't manage after all, eh? Not so easy, is it, when all's said and done, doing for yerself and earning yer living. I ain't saying a word, mind, but you 'ad a good 'ome, my girl. All I'm saying is, I hopes you're satisfied, because you upset your mum and me very bad, going off like you did."

Mum brought the big teapot slowly to the table and sat down. "You're arsting to come 'ome, I s'pose," she said, without looking at Cheryl, and giving nothing away.

"No I ain't!" said Cheryl.

"Well, what is it, then?" said Dad.

"I come to arst — " She stopped, and then started again in a small voice, "I got nothink for the rent. I'll pay you back, after Christmas, when I gets me new job."

There was a long silence, then Dad said: "I never said a word. Skint, eh? What'd I tell you, then? It don't surprise me one bit. What makes you think we got anythink for you, after the way you treated us?"

"Please, Dad. Just a little." Cheryl's voice cracked. "Just over Christmas till I'm earning again."

"Now look here, my girl!" Dad emphasized each word with a jab of his horny, brown-stained forefinger. "Let this be a lesson to you. I ain't cruel, but you gotta learn. I works 'ard for my lot, I does, and you better start doing the same. You don't get nothink free these days. If you're broke you'll 'ave to go on the Assistance, my girl; they can afford to keep you better'n what I can."

Cheryl looked aghast. "I am, Dad — I am on it! It ain't enough, see — not to cover the rent, and food, and

159

things for the baby."

"You'll just 'ave to cut down on your ideas, then, won't you? I've 'ad to learn you can't 'ave everything. 'Ave to cut down on some luxuries — paint for yer face and dance dresses and the like — same as all of us these days."

"I don't have no — " Cheryl began, but he held up his hand for silence.

"I 'ates to be 'ard, but it's kinder in the end. I spoilt you once, and look what 'appened. I ain't giving in, for yer own good, and that's me last word on the subject."

Cheryl looked from one to the other of them, but no one met her eyes. "Where's Deb?" she said at last.

"Gone downstairs to Purdies for the afternoon," Marilyn told her, without looking up.

Cheryl snorted.

"That what she tell you? And you all believed her? Know what I think? I think she run away like me, 'cos she couldn't bear it no longer here. And I'll tell you summink else — I'll bet our Kev run away too — I'll bet all the kids'll run away, just to get away from you, and one day you'll be all alone, just the two of you wiv no one to go at but each other, and serve you flipping well right, and I hopes yer downright miserable!"

"'Ave you quite finished?" said Dad. "You satisfied now? Look at yer mum. Look what you done to 'er. Marilyn! Go downstairs at once and tell Debra to come up this instant if she don't want me to take the strap to her backside. No, wait!" He lumbered to his feet. "You stay 'ere and look after your mother. I'm going down meself to fetch her back."

"Oh my gosh, Mr Webster!" said Debbie, relief

160

flooding round her like a warm bath. "You din't 'arf give me a turn!"

He lit a large, powerful torch and walked towards her. She couldn't see him behind the light but the sound of his firm tread was infinitely reassuring.

"I thought," said Mr Webster, without sounding very severe about it, "that I told you not to come here. Where's Marilyn?"

"At home," said Debbie. "She don't know I'm here. But you knows why I had to come."

"But you haven't found your friend?" he said.

"Huh!" said Debbie. "Friend! He flippin' near found me, though! Cor — you was right, sir — so was the fuzz an' all. 'E's dangerous all right. And barmy as they come. Chased me 'arf round the houses, he did! I'm lucky to be alive — I'm telling you the honest!"

"I believe you, Debbie," he said gravely.

"I give him the slip though," Debbie went on, proudly. "There's one thing — if he's in that house in there, we got him. He can't get — " She stopped, remembering the stranger's uncanny ability to get in or out of any situation. It seemed to be his stock in trade. She shivered, suddenly realising how bitterly cold it was. "I ain't half glad you're here sir," she said.

"How did you know you could get through the wall back into here?" asked Mr Webster.

"I seen that hole once before," Debbie admitted. "Then when I were in the other house I got the same whiff and that reminded me. I knows that pong — not them joss sticks, but like burning leaves and that."

"Do you mean cannabis?" said Mr Webster.

"Eh?"

"Cannabis. Perhaps you know it as pot or grass or even weed?"

161

"Yeah, that," said Debbie. She had smelt it in the derelict houses, she had smelt it once or twice at school, and she had smelt it somewhere else recently, but still she couldn't remember where. "Someone's been 'aving a few joints down here," she added, to impress him with her worldly knowledge.

"Seems like it," he agreed. "They were lucky to get out alive."

"Go on!" said Debbie. "Pot ain't dangerous."

"Dangerous enough to be illegal."

"That's stupid," said Debbie, trotting out the half-heard phrases of older children. "It only makes you feel good — it don't even make you high like speed."

"Even drowsiness can be dangerous. It spoils your concentration. Think of trying to cross a busy road, let alone find your way safely out of this building, if your mind's all woozy with drugs. Besides, drugs are a habit — an astonishingly quick one, too. You smoke a joint or two and the world seems a better place for it — so you do it more often, and make it stronger, and blot out your real, uncomfortable, difficult life with its challenges and problems. And all the time you don't realise it's making you dopier and dopier and more and more of a failure, instead of helping you get on better. And then one day someone offers you something stronger — a much bigger kick that makes pot-smoking seem like chocolate cigarettes — and after that, if the first time doesn't kill you, it's only a matter of time."

Debbie's mind was working overtime while he was talking.

"Hey, where do they get their stuff from — what they smokes in their joints?"

"That's what's called the sixty-four thousand dollar question, Debbie. If the police knew that they'd stand a

162

better chance of putting a stop to it. A drug-taker knows a peddler, who has his supplier, who is in touch with someone who imports it. Why do you ask?"

"Because," said Debbie, excitedly, "I think I knows where this lot gets theirs from. Come over 'ere and see what I found."

She grabbed the flashlight from him and led the way to the hole through which she had climbed. "Look in there, sir! See? All them little parcels — 'undreds of 'em — I couldn't think what they was, but now I guessed! That's pot, ain't it, waiting to be smoked!"

There was a long pause while Mr Webster obediently looked along the beam of light into the gap between the walls.

"No, Debbie," he said at last. "I'm afraid that's not cannabis." He sounded almost as disappointed as she felt.

"You sure? You ain't looked inside. . . . What is it then?"

"That is the big one. That, Debbie, is the big kick, the something stronger that changes the world we know into a fantasy of dreams and visions. I only wish to God you hadn't found it."

"But why? What is it?"

"It is usually known as acid. The real name is LSD. This is the biggest haul of the stuff that I have ever seen."

"LSD? That's what my auntie took when she went mad." But that hadn't looked like this . . . .

Mr Webster knelt down and felt about among the little parcels. "Some of it's already made up into tablets, look. The rest's powder." He went on as though he were talking to himself: "Just a few grains to each dose; multiply that by the number in each packet . . . multiply that by the number of packets. . . . Thousands upon thousands of pounds — it could run into hundreds of thousands. Enough to liberate a poor school master from the classroom and set him up in luxury for ever."

Debbie hardly heard him. If there were tablets here as well, then this must be where Joe had got the stuff. No wonder he had laughed when Marilyn had said the sweet looked like an acid drop. "Where'd it come from?" she asked. "'Oo's it?"

"Where it came from originally, I don't know. As for who owns it, that's a very complicated question. There are so many cogs in a wheel of this kind: some very big, some so small they know nothing about the machine they help to make tick. Every time the stuff changes hands someone involved gets his rake-off, so in one sense it has many owners, but you wouldn't find a soul who'd claim it if it came to a question of law."

"But why's it here?" said Debbie, still completely mystified.

There was a pause, then Mr Webster said, "I'll tell you what I think happened. I think it has been delivered here to be picked up by someone else in the circle and redistributed in smaller quantities. But somewhere along the line something went wrong with the machine. A cog has slipped out of place and the wheels have ceased to turn. And as a result, the stuff is still hidden here."

Joe, thought Debbie. He was the small cog that had slipped out of place — down the basement stairs in fact — so that he had been unable to keep the machine moving.

Mr Webster asked suddenly, "Did Kevin ever come here by himself, without you and Marilyn, do you know?"

"Once or twice, maybe," said Debbie, cautiously. "Why?"

164

"Because one day last week we had some carpentry wood pinched from school and Kevin was convinced he'd seen it nailed across the way into one of these houses. Whether he was right or not doesn't matter; the point is, Kevin had been close enough to recognise it. And the next day he disappeared. I think whoever should have received the drugs saw Kevin nosing around and knew, or at least suspected, that he had seen too much. Kevin had to be removed in case he blew the whistle on the whole thing."

Debbie nodded in the darkness. It was all beginning to fall into place at last. Kevin had certainly nosed round on his own and seen things no one had been meant to find. The cog that had slipped out of place knew that he knew too much. . . . But on the day Kevin had been there alone Joe had been unconscious, and when he saw him again she and Marilyn had been there too, and Joe would have had no more reason to kidnap Kevin than any of them. She reckoned the time had come to tell Mr Webster about Joe.

"We ain't the first to find the acid," she said. "There was this feller we met here; he got some. It were him what give me the one as Auntie Lil nicked out of me pocket and ate."

"Who did? That man Angel or whatever his name is, the police are after?"

"No, not the old bloke. This boy. We finds him in the basement."

She heard him suck his breath in sharply through his teeth. "You never told me all this," he said roughly.

Debbie was instantly defensive. "Why should I? It were our business."

She expected him to be angry, and braced herself for the coming reprimand, but when he spoke he did not seem to have noticed any impertinence.

"Why did Joe give you the sweet, Debbie?"

"We brung him some things he wanted."

"Brought," said Mr Webster, automatically. "Yes, of course, the thermos and the sandwiches — they were quite fresh. I should have guessed — I might have known . . . "

"Sir," said Debbie suddenly, "who was *meant* to find it?"

"The pusher. The man who persuades other people to buy and use the stuff."

"Crumbs!" said Debbie. "He can't never 'ave seen what it do, then. No one couldn't want people to go like our auntie did. 'Ere!" she exclaimed excitedly — "Betcher it were that mad angel — 'e's crazy as they come, look!"

"No, Debbie. No, I don't think your angel fellow's a drug-pusher. Anyone in that line of business has to be very sane indeed. You have to be hard-headed with nerves of iron to work for an organisation of that sort, or you just go under and get rubbed out."

"But s'posing he'd took some, like Auntie Lil. That might've sent him soft in the head like her."

"Pushers don't take the stuff themselves, Debbie. Only fools do that. The pushers' part is to sell it to people stupid enough to buy it. If a drug-pusher became a drug-taker he'd never live long enough to enjoy his very considerable fortune. That would indeed be madness."

Debbie shivered. If he were right in his reasoning there were people about — quite sane, sensible people — who deliberately made money out of the hideous, nightmarish misery of others.

"Sir — can we go 'ome now?" she said. "I'm getting ever so cold and tired stood here. Besides, no one don't know I'm here and I'm gonna get into trouble for

166

stopping out late."

"I have a feeling, Debbie, you never spoke a truer word," he said. "But first of all you and I have just one more little job to do. Come with me."

She put her hand in his, gladly, thankful to feel the comforting pressure in the loneliness of the house. He led her out into the hall and began to walk upstairs. He had explained a great deal to her, but there was still a lot she did not understand. How, for instance, had he known Joe's name? What was he doing in the house himself, instead of going away for Christmas that day after all? Why had he wished she had not found the LSD? And where on earth was he taking her now?

They rounded the bend after the first floor, the flashlight's powerful beam revealing the trap door leading to the attic ahead.

"Sir," said Debbie, "if Joe see us lot in here, why'd he pick on our Kev? And if that daft angel ain't the pusher, what did he want in here anyway?"

She thought she could feel him smiling as he gripped her hand more tightly in the darkness.

"As far as Joe is concerned, he is such a *very* small cog he merely obeys the pusher's instructions — indeed, to do anything else is probably more than his life is worth." He paused to grasp her firmly with one arm while he reached up with the other and pulled down the ring-handled door. "To answer your second question, there has been only one man here with you this afternoon, Debbie, and he, though quite sane and sober, is no angel. And it's no use struggling, my dear, even if you have put two and two together at last, because your touching faith in me has made it all as easy as — dare I say it? — taking sweets from a child! You see, as Kevin inadvertently warned me and you have just obligingly confirmed, the trouble is that you three know too much. So you are going to spend another little session up here while I get the stuff out of the house, only this time there will be no running away as you have destroyed your only escape route. After that, if a very serious and tragic accident hasn't already occurred, then I shall have to come and see to it myself. The fact of the matter is that the big bad wolf is after you lot, Debbie, and he's just caught the second little pig!"

EIGHTEEN

Mrs Purdie was indignant at the suggestion that she had been harbouring Debbie all afternoon.

"Sure and I haven't set eyes on none o' your kids for more'n a week now, Mr Williamson," she protested tearfully. "My Bernadette has gone out shopping as nice as could be with her Auntie Maureen — "

"I don't care where your Bernadette gone," Dad interrupted her. "It's my Debra I wants. She tell me as she was coming down to your place and I ain't leaving till I got her."

"Oh no, no, Mr Williamson!" Mrs Purdie wept. "Ye'll be after wakin' my Michael any minute! Holy Mother of God, that'll be him now!"

The bedroom door opened, revealing Mr Purdie. He was hardly taller than Dad, but great knotted muscles stood out on his copper-coloured arms, and a rusty luxuriance billowed out above the scarlet blanket knotted round his middle. The bull neck bent slightly as little sleep-reddened eyes focused upon his visitor. Mr Purdie gave a low snort and advanced a few sideways steps, his fists clenched . . . .

Dad apologised for the intrusion and retreated rapidly upstairs where he dropped into his chair by the fireside. He said heavily, "She ain't there."

"What d'you mean," said Mum, "she ain't there?"

"Just what I says, don't I?" said Dad. "Can't put it no plainer. She ain't wiv Purdies, nor never 'as bin."

"Well where is she, then?" said Mum. "Ain't you find

169

her?"

"No I ain't," said Dad. "And what's more, I dunno wheres to look. Gorn, ain't she — run away, most like, just like Cheryl said. First Terry, look, then Cheryl, then Kevin, now our Debra."

"Oh Dad — I din't mean — I never thought — " Cheryl sniffed, her mouth working. Marilyn's face, too, had begun to pucker.

Mum gave Stephen and Carole each a bag of crisps without looking at either of them, her face expressing nothing. "Best get the police, Les," she said at last.

The inspector was sympathetic but nonplussed. He addressed most of his questions to Marilyn: not only was she closest to Debbie but she was in the fittest state to answer them.

"Did Debbie often go downstairs to play with Bernadette Purdie?"

"No." Marilyn buttered a slice of bread and put jam on it.

"Just sometimes, eh?"

"No. She never went before."

"I see. Did she suggest you went with her?"

"No." Marilyn took a large bite and said through it, "She knows I ain't partic'lar about Bernadette."

The inspector said suddenly, "Do you think she ever meant to spend the afternoon downstairs?"

Marilyn shrugged. "Wouldn't like to say."

"Supposing she didn't," said the inspector. "Supposing she made Bernadette an excuse to get out, where d'you think she might have gone?"

"Dunno. She never tell me nothink."

"Where do you two girls go when you go out together?"

"You must be joking!" Marilyn licked her fingers and

glared balefully at Mum. "We never hardly goes out."

"Hardly ever in, you mean," Mum retorted. "Worry me to death, you two does." She turned to the inspector. "They was at the cinema only yesterday."

"Just the two of you?" he asked Marilyn.

"No. We was took by one of our teachers."

"That was nice of her, wasn't it?"

"Him, you mean. You don't think the Cow'd do nothink like that."

"Who?"

"Mrs Cowan. That's our teacher. Mr Webster's Kev's."

"And he took you?"

"Yeah. He's dishy."

"I see. And did he suggest any further meetings or anything?"

"No. He went away for Christmas today, see."

"And you can't think of anything he said that might give us an idea of where Debbie could be?"

"No. I only knows one place where she won't be."

"Where's that?"

"The bomb site."

"I'm glad to hear it," said the inspector drily. "But what makes you so sure?"

Marilyn thought for a minute, shifting her feet uneasily under the table. There was a bruise on her shin where Debbie had kicked her for saying too much the day before. She rubbed it ruefully and said, "Mr Webster tell us not to, that's why."

"Any particular reason?" The inspector sounded casual, almost uninterested.

Marilyn hesitated. She would have been black and blue by now if Debbie had been there. "He said as how he see that angel feller there who prob'ly knows a thing or two about our Kev."

171

The inspector was staring at her. "Go on. What else did he say?"

"I — I dunno. I can't remember." Marilyn was frightened. She had said more than she meant already.

"Try to, Marilyn. This could be very important."

"MARILYN!" shouted Mum and Dad in unison, and Dad added, "You just remember what he said this instant, my girl. Or else."

"He said — he said — "

Marilyn searched wildly in her imagination for what Debbie would have said, had she been there.

"Well?" said the inspector, encouragingly.

There was a brief, expectant silence, then Marilyn with a helpless wail of "I dunno", burst into tears.

The young man in the bar of the Kendal Arms sighed deeply.

"What's up, mate?" said his neighbour. "Won't she 'ave you?"

"Seems like no one won't," said the younger one bitterly.

"Why's that, then?"

"I've fell out wiv me folks, see . . ." He hesitated. "Everyone's against me, look. Anywheres I goes, I ain't bin there no time before they pushes me out again."

The older man looked at him shrewdly. "Fuzz, eh?" he remarked.

"Yeah. Them too. They're all against me, I tells you."

"What they want you for then, eh?"

The young man seemed irritated by the question. "I dunno, do I? Ain't done nothink so far as I know."

"Why don't you arst 'em, then?" the other suggested.

"Look, I don't want no trouble, see. Even if I ain't done nothink, they'll find summink to pin on me,

172

won't they? So I reckon I'll just keep outa their way, see."

The older man shrugged his shoulders and pointed to the television set in the corner. "News coming on," he said. "They still ain't found that kid yet. Reckon he's still alive?"

The young man glanced up and then stared at the screen in astonishment. "'Ere!" he said at last. "That's my kid brother there, would you believe?"

The other finished his beer and set down the mug with deliberation.

"Know what I think, mate?" he said. "I think you got one of them 'ang-ups. Know what I mean — you thinks the whole world's down on you. Same as the wife's mother — she thinks that. Under the doctor for it, she is, 'as to take tablets for it an' all. You can't 'elp it, son, but that's a right 'ang-up you got there, an' no mistake."

The picture on the screen changed from a small boy to a larger girl.

"There y'are, look!" said the older man. "S'pose you be telling me next that's yer kid sister, too."

There was no mistaking the thick fringe with the round, bright eyes beneath it.

"Yeah!" said the young man, slowly. "Yeah — that's her an' all . . . ."

"You oughter see a doc, mate, and get him to give you summink — "

But the young man was not listening. He got up and walked out into the street. Ten minutes later he came to a forbidding stone building with a blue light over the door. He walked up the steps, through the swing doors and across to a desk where a uniformed man was sitting.

"Terence Williamson," he said.

*

Mr Webster stopped with one foot on the bottom rung of the folding ladder. Someone was moving about in the darkness down below. Debbie, seizing her opportunity, emitted a piercing scream for help. Immediately Mr Webster's hand covered her mouth tightly and he whispered in her ear, "If you so much as move a muscle you'll be over the top in less time than it takes to tell about it."

She believed him: a man who could do what he had confessed to would not stop at helping anyone to a rapid end over those broken bannisters. They both listened intently but there was silence again downstairs. Mr Webster swung the beam of the torch over the staircase, picking out a slight figure with a bandaged ankle in the hall beneath them.

"What the devil are you doing here?" he called out. "I told you not to come here till I sent for you."

Joe put his hands on his hips and looked insolently upwards into the light. "I ain't doing no more baby-sitting for the likes of you," he said. "There's too many questions being arsted round my pad."

Mr Webster drew in his breath sharply; Debbie could feel his mounting anger at her back.

"What've you done with the kid then? I shall see to it you take full responsibility if anything's happened to him."

"You'll be lucky," Joe sneered. "You got two of 'em on your hands now, look."

There was a sudden crashing and banging downstairs, followed presently by men's voices in the region of the front door. Someone called out, "Debbie! Are you in here somewhere?"

Instantly Mr Webster's grip tightened round her mouth till her teeth dug into her lip and the skin under

174

her eyes felt stretched and sore. Downstairs the voices and the tramping feet drew nearer and receded again into each room in turn.

Very quietly Mr Webster began to inch his way backwards up the attic steps, practically carrying Debbie. She went along with him to the best of her ability: if she stumbled she might alert whoever was downstairs, but that would not help her much if he carried out his threat.

Suddenly the steps gave an ominous creak and gave an inch or two. Immediately a blinding light from a powerful torch shone full in their faces. Someone called out, "There she is!" and the inspector's voice shouted, "Stop! Come on down, you there!"

Mr Webster moved up one more step and there was a hurried conversation downstairs. Debbie caught the words, "That's him . . . school teacher . . . other child somewhere . . . ."

"All right, Webster!" the Inspector called out. "Just let her go and come down quietly."

Debbie began again to struggle, but he kept his hold upon her. "One move in this direction," he warned them, "and the kid's had it."

He took another step upwards; Debbie with him.

"Webster!" rapped out the inspector. "You can't get away with this!"

Mr Webster retreated another step and the staircase creaked loudly again. Debbie wondered hopefully whether it would collapse beneath the weight of them both. It would be a lot less far to fall than the whole height of the main stairs.

"Don't come any nearer!" commanded Mr Webster. "I mean it when I say I'll throw her over to you." He heaved Debbie up with him again.

There were more whispers downstairs and then the inspector voiced Debbie's own thoughts: "What do you intend to do?"

Mr Webster gave a short laugh. "You can find that out for yourselves when I've gone," he replied.

"You won't get far," said the inspector.

"You don't think so?"

Mr Webster backed up another step. They were nearly at the top now, and still the inspector showed no sign of being in any sort of control of the situation as far as Debbie could see. It was all very well to stand there and keep him talking, but this was not stopping him. Once inside the attic and they would be out of sight as well as out of reach, with the sheer drop from the rooftop or the inside of the next house between themselves and the outside world.

"Webster!" shouted the inspector, "I must warn you, the house is surrounded!"

"Sure. And I'm warning you that the girl comes too, and at the first move from one of your men to stop me she goes over the top, and that's a long way for a kid to fall."

He took a last step off the top rung into the attic, and in a moment of frenzied determination Debbie managed to open her mouth just wide enough to admit the fleshy bit of his hand between his forefinger and thumb. There was a sickening crunch as her front teeth met, and a howl of pain and rage from Mr Webster. The next thing Debbie knew she was lying at the bottom of the attic steps and people were bending over her asking if she was all right. She sat up, bruised, dazed — and free.

"Good girl!" the inspector was saying. "You timed that lovely. We'll have you in the force yet. Not hurt, are you?"

Debbie gingerly accepted several helping hands up off the floor. "I'm OK," she said. "Where is he?"

"On his way to the station. We had a few of our men hiding up in that attic, waiting to nab him when he arrived. That nip you gave him just took his attention at the right moment. Your brother Terry, here, took 'em round and showed 'em the way in while I kept him talking round this side."

"Terry?" She looked round, wondering if she had heard him rightly. "Terry! What you doing here?"

"Hi, Deb!" He emerged from the shadows, curly-maned and saucy as ever. Debbie sniffed the air — and realised suddenly whom she had been trying to remember: the person connected with that downstairs room, who had the smell of cannabis upon him, clinging in his leather jacket and his hair.

"Well stone me!" she said. "Our Terry, would you believe! 'Ere!" She jerked a thumb towards the inspector. "They wanted you, din't they? What's it all about then? What you done, eh?"

Terry smiled a confident, sardonic smile. "Yeah, well you see it were that bloke I worked for up at the garage, weren't it. 'E never oughter've sell me that bike, see, it weren't 'is in the first place, like. So the cops was trying to trace him, and one of me mates tells 'em I worked there, but I gone by that time, hadn't I?"

Debbie nodded, satisfied, if not fully understanding. One thing was clear: Terry was not in any trouble with the police. It had been something quite innocent to do with his motor-bike — Kevin had been right after all. She turned to the inspector.

"Ain't you found our Kev yet?"

The inspector said with studied cheerfulness: "That's

177

what we've got to get cracking on again next. We've found you, anyhow, and the sooner we get you home the better; your parents are frantic enough about you as it is."

Debbie allowed herself to be led carefully downstairs. In the hall she stopped. "Don't you want to see where them drugs is first?" she said. "What Mr Webster come for?"

The policemen exchanged glances and looked back at her again.

"What drugs, Debbie? What d'you mean?"

"In 'ere, look."

She opened the door and pulled the inspector after her, flashlight and all. There was a sudden movement by the opposite wall.

"Stop him! Quick!" shouted the inspector.

There was a brief scuffle and the culprit stood before them, blinking in the torchlight, a bulging canvas bag in his hand. The inspector looked inside and caught his breath.

"All right," he said. "Take him in. We'll get the details at the station."

"'Ang about!" said Debbie as the man moved off. "That there's Joe. He were here with Mr Webster when you come. He knows where our Kev is. Go on, get the screws on him — make him tell you!"

Joe's eyes avoided all of them. He said nothing.

"Well?" said the inspector sharply. "It'll go easier for you if you co-operate, you know."

Joe shuffled his feet between the two constables. "I din't mean the kid no harm," he whined. "That there Webster made me nab him so he could grab that one and find out 'ow much they know about the stuff. He never say I was to keep him all that time, and he

178

hollered till the neighbours started arsting questions. I couldn't keep him no longer, see, and I had to do summink, see. I had that Webster on me back, din't I, threatening 'e'd blow me to you fellers about this job if anyone rumbled the kid — "

"Where is he?" the inspector interrupted sternly. "Where's the boy now?"

Joe looked sullen. "I 'ad to do it, see. I 'ad to do summink wiv him, din't I? I 'ad to keep him quiet, see." He pointed at his feet. "He's down there."

Debbie darted to the basement door, wrenching Kevin's torch from her raincoat pocket.

"Debbie, stop!" called the inspector. "Stop her, one of you! Don't let her go down there!"

One of the constables was after her, but the tiny light had come to tenuous life again, just enabling her to grope her way down in the darkness.

"Come back, missie," urged the policeman. "Let me come past — don't go down there, there's a good girl!"

But Debbie hardly heard him. If Kevin had been down there all this time, why hadn't he shouted? And what had Joe meant when he said he had meant him no harm but he had "had to do something"? She didn't really want to know or to find out, but something forced her on and on down that dark and difficult stairway, on into the room that used to be the kitchen — and there in front of her was the angel, and on his knee lay Kevin, sleeping like a baby.

NINETEEN

The doctor said that Kevin must be encouraged to talk about his experience: it would help him not to have any delayed reaction. Kevin needed no encouragement.

"There was these two blokes with that Joe, see," he explained for the umpteenth time. "An' they just nabbed me while Mr Webster was looking the other way. He were standing right between me and the other kids so no one see what happened."

"He done that on purpose," said Debbie, wisely.

"Course he ain't!" Kevin scoffed. "It were that Joe what grabbed me, not our Mr Webster!"

Debbie appealed to the inspector.

"I'm afraid she's right," he agreed. "Your Mr Webster organised it all. You see, Joe was supposed to report to him that the drugs had been delivered, take his reward and get lost, but the silly idiot went and tasted one. As you know very well, some of the stuff was already made up into tablets. He was luckier than your auntie; he only fell downstairs, where first he was found unconscious by Kevin, and then later by all of you. Meanwhile Webster was going frantic, thinking Joe had made off with the lot, and was bound to get caught, and far from making a packet out of it they'd all go to chokey. Eventually he became so desperate he stepped out of line himself and went to see what had happened. He found Joe in a pretty ropey state, his excuse being that he'd fallen downstairs while waiting for the drugs which had never arrived — presumably because of the unexpected weather

180

conditions. Webster suspected that he'd been on a trip and that therefore the drugs were there somewhere, and that Joe intended coming back to collar the lot. It was then that he hit on the idea of grabbing everything for himself and framing Joe who was already up to his neck in the same trouble. He knew one word from him in the right place would sign Joe's death warrant promptly. So he pretended to believe Joe and helped him out of the building, returning immediately to bar up the way in to prevent anyone getting in before he'd had a chance to return himself. Only one thing bothered him: he'd seen you three playing around those houses — and incidentally, you had seen him — and he did not know how much you knew. That was why he took some of the same wood he had used to cover the entrance — the other half of the same packing case — to school, to see if you, Kevin, recognised it, which of course you did."

"Blimey!" said Kevin. "Were he the thief all the time what pinched our wood?"

"He certainly was, Kevin. And from what you said to him he realised you not only knew more than was safe but that Debbie was away from school with a cold — at large to find out more, or even give the game away to the police."

Debbie turned on Kevin. "Hey — what'd you go tellin' him?"

"Nuffink." Kevin shut his mouth and glared at her defensively.

"Exactly," said the inspector. "It was your very silence on the matter which made him suspicious. If you had indeed known nothing you'd have been asking every question under the sun. As it was, Webster had to remove you from the scene while he grabbed the drugs — and at the same time distract attention from his own

181

manoeuvres. So he ordered Joe to kidnap you, Kevin, and guard you, knowing Joe wouldn't dare disobey and would be kept occupied well away from the houses. If he got away with it, Kevin would never have known Webster had been responsible — as he clearly didn't. Webster then booked a flight to Switzerland after Christmas, under another name. Your headmaster would have had a letter saying he'd had a very bad ski-ing accident and wouldn't be able to come back next term, if ever. From there he was off to Australia to start a new life and spend his ill-gotten gains. So far, so good, but from then on everything started to go wrong for him. First of all, your auntie was taken violently ill with LSD. Webster reckoned she must have got it from one of you, so therefore you had found the haul and Joe had been lying. He also knew that we would now try to connect this with Kevin's kidnapping and start fishing around for the rest of those tablets. And to add to his worries, your elusive friend Angel appeared on the scene, claiming to know more than anyone about the whole thing. Goodness only knew what he might have seen or heard, let alone whom he might tell.

"Webster was convinced Angel was another rival for the drugs and it could have been him who had given you the one your auntie took. There was only one thing for it: Webster had to get them out as fast as he could before we got onto him. But — he didn't know where Joe had hidden the stuff. You, Debbie, he felt pretty certain, did. At least he figured you knew enough to lead him to the right place. So he took you and Marilyn out to tea and hinted heavily that you might find a clue to Kevin's whereabouts at the houses. Then he dropped another hint that he would be safely out of the way — then I gather he more or less dared you to go there. Then,

182

his trap laid, he took you home, proving himself a reliable friend of the family.

"Well, of course, his plan didn't work. You didn't know where the drugs were, and up till the time when you actually took him and showed them to him, he still had no idea what you had seen. He had decided to cut his losses, pretend that he had come to keep an eye on you in case you came looking for Kevin, and rely on your extreme reluctance to tell the police anything at all to keep the little escapade secret from us."

"Why'd he shut me in the attic then?" said Debbie, with feeling.

"He was playing for time. He wanted to be sure he knew where to come and look before it was quite dark. Clearly, you knew nothing useful after all, and he could safely have 'rescued' you when he was ready, pretending to check for himself that Kevin wasn't there before he went away. There would have been an unbreakable pact of silence between you: he would undertake to keep quiet that you had been there; you could not have split on him without giving yourself away. But you escaped and showed him everything. Worse than that — you told him about your meeting with Joe. That did it. Once he knew you three connected Kevin's kidnapper with the drugs it was only a matter of time before you blew him to us, after which it was a short step to you lot coming clean and giving away his own involvement.

"I think it was at that moment that he finally panicked. You know what he had planned for you, Debbie, and I think it would have been a long time before you were found. Then he was going to get the drugs away and split on Joe to the underworld, who would certainly have sent a professional thug along to murder him quietly and without trace."

The children gazed at him, awestruck.

"What about our Kev?" said Debbie. "What would've 'appened to him?"

The inspector looked at them for a moment and then said quietly, "I wouldn't have given a fig for his chances. He knew about the drugs and he knew about Joe and he would have known quite enough for us to bring a murder charge against someone. I think there's no doubt he would have gone the same way as Joe."

There was dead silence while they took this in. Then Debbie said, "How d'you know all this, eh?"

"Both Webster and Joe have already made very full statements. The law is always more lenient on people who confess with no trouble. But you know, I think in Webster's case remorse played its part. The odd thing is that in spite of it all he's a born schoolmaster and really quite fond of you all. The tragedy of his life is that he loves money more than anything else in the world: more than his career, more than peace of mind — more even than human life. So when you lot threatened his ambitions you had to go in case you stopped him getting away with all that money."

"What about Lyn?" said Debbie. "Was he gonna knock her off too?"

"He wouldn't have been above it," admitted the inspector, "but in fact he hadn't intended to stay long enough for that. After all, Marilyn didn't know about the drugs or even that you had gone to the houses. You told him yourself no one knew where you were. No, I think he relied on Marilyn being too shaken to say anything useful, which in fact was quite unfounded because she gave us the initial clue as to where you might be."

"What made you go to them houses when you did?" said Debbie.

184

"Well," said the inspector, "it was a clue here and a clue there that suddenly added up. Finally, your brother Terry suddenly walked into the station and asked us what we wanted him for. Well, having sorted out the little matter of the motor-bike, he said had we looked for you two in the derelict houses. Then he came clean and admitted that he'd been in on a few pot parties in one of them and didn't want any questions asked. Then it all came out how he and you, Debbie had tried to get in last week, and that the first time he'd gone to meet you our Mr Webster had mysteriously prevented him. So we began to see his part in all this, and also that there might be developments at those houses since our men had searched for Kevin there. And of course the entrance had been unbarred again. So we got Terry to take a few of our men up by the roof while we broke in down below, and sure enough — well you know the rest."

"Cor!" said Kevin. "Our Mr Webster — a crook! It don't seem possible somehow."

Mum pursed her lips. "It do to me. I never did trust 'im. I never did want 'im to take you girls out, but you would go. Always know best, you two do, and look! P'raps next time you'll listen to me for once."

Debbie changed the subject quickly. "Kev — how'd you get into that basement without me hearing you then?"

"That Joe brung me. He sez I were going home, see. He give me a cuppa tea what tasted queer and then he sticks a bit of plaster over me mouth before I sees what's coming, and shoves this balaclava over me head so no one don't see I got me mouth stuck up. Then he takes me to them houses and 'arf carries me down there I'm that tired, and next thing I knows I'm layin' on the floor and our Deb's shouting in me ear."

185

"Poor lamb!" said Mum, but Debbie corrected him.

"No you wasn't laying on no floor! You was on that angel's lap — I seen him!"

"Don't talk so daft," said Kevin. "He weren't there."

Debbie looked round for support, but first the inspector and then Terry shook their heads, denying seeing anyone but Kevin.

Mum got to her feet. "I'll get yer supper, duck," she told Kevin. "Beans on toast, eh?"

Kevin made a face. "Oh no, Mum! That Joe give me nothink else. Can I 'ave one of them mince pies?"

"Ah, bless him!" said Mum. "You can have 'em all, son. I made 'em for Lil really — she don't mind a mince pie — but I can do some more for 'er."

"Blimey!" whispered Debbie to Marilyn. "You gotta be half dead to get anythink in this place."

The inspector put down his teacup and stood up. "I must be getting home," he said. "My own children will be waiting to hang up their stockings when I come."

"Stockings!" said Debbie. "Is it Christmas tomorrow?"

"It certainly is, young lady," said the inspector. "And I'll confess it now — there were moments when I never thought I'd be wishing you all a happy one."

"I got nothink ready!" wailed Mum. "Not even a chicken! It didn't seem right somehow . . ."

"I'll get you one, Mum," said Terry. "I'll get you a turkey if you like. I'll get you one what fell — " He caught the inspector's eye. "I knows a feller what sells 'em cheap to friends," he said.

Mum looked doubtful. "Won't have to be froze," she said. "Never get it done in time."

"No Mum — fresh — honest!"

The children went down to the street door with the inspector.

"Under the circumstances," he said, "I'm not going to take any action over your part in all this. I accept that you did not steal that tablet and that you did not intend your auntie or anyone else to swallow it. But I think you will admit you are not wholly innocent in this matter."

They admitted it.

"Good," said the inspector. "Then I think that you and your mum and dad have been punished enough, and all I need to do is to urge you all to turn over a new leaf in the future. I'm happy to say I shan't have to trust you for very long because that whole square has now been condemned and is due to be demolished after Christmas."

"Cor!" said Debbie. "What they gonna put there instead?"

"Modern blocks of flats," said the inspector. "No more opportunities for hiding or even trespassing."

"Blimey!" said Kevin, as the full implication struck him. "They got a flipping nerve! Where they think we gonna play then?"

The inspector sighed. "Hyde Park is very pleasant, I believe," he said. Then he wished them a happy Christmas and shook hands with each in turn, telling Debbie she was a very courageous young lady, but that he did hope she would not go looking for any more adventures for a long, long time to come.

On their way upstairs again Kevin said, "Look, there's someone stood by our front door!"

"Don't be daft," said Marilyn. "We'd have passed 'em on the way down."

"He's right, though!" said Debbie. "It's our angel, look!" She began running up the remaining stairs two at at time.

187

They pushed him into the flat ahead of them. "Mum! Dad! It's our angel come — the one what saved our Kev and tell Auntie Lil everythink's gonna be OK!"

Mum wiped floury hands on her apron and said, "Pleased to meet you, I'm sure, Mr Angel." Dad shook hands with him and even offered him a chair by the fire. The children gathered round, delighted that their special friend should be accepted by the family. Even Stephen and Carole, still awake with all the excitement, treated him like an old friend.

"Stopping long?" Dad asked. "Yer welcome if you wants to."

The angel thanked him courteously, but said he was expected at his own home for Christmas.

"Far to go?" said Dad.

"No distance at all," the angel assured him.

"What's your 'ome like?" asked Debbie, curiously.

"Very like yours tonight."

"Like ours?" She looked round in amazement at the chipped and peeling paintwork and the shabby furniture. "Go on!" she said.

"Not to look at, maybe," said the angel, "but in other respects, very like."

"Like to try one of me mince pies, Mr Angel?" said Mum. "Hot from the oven, look."

"Thank you very much," said the angel, with a glance at Debbie that dared her to say he neither ate nor drank.

"I'm just making a few for me sister," Mum explained. "I'm going over to see her tomorrow — well, I mean it ain't very good being in 'ospital over Christmas." She looked up suddenly, recognition dawning in her eyes. "Oh, of course, you knows her, don't you — that policeman sez you and her had a few words outside here the night she had her accident."

188

"Sweet on her, ain't you," said Dad, in a voice which implied that there was no accounting for tastes.

"My dear sir," said the angel, without rancour, "while it is always a pleasure to help anyone, I must point out that your sister-in-law has the exceedingly doubtful distinction of being the first person in many thousands of years ever to have told an angel from heaven to get knotted."

He finished his mince pie and took his leave, asking permission for the children to come a little way to see him off. Debbie was surprised at the readiness with which this was granted, but then he always had been a dab hand at getting his own way.

Outside a thin drizzle was falling.

"Don't it feel warm?" said Kevin. "It weren't 'arf cold at that Joe's."

"It's thawring," said Marilyn.

Debbie looked at Kevin. Then she took the angel's arm affectionately.

"You was there with our Kev really in that basement, wasn't you?" she said. "I know I seen you, din't I?"

"I am," said the angel, "amongst many other things, a fully qualified guardian. It's all part of my job. But there are some people who have eyes and see nothing with them all their lives."

"Then how'm I to tell 'em it ain't me what's seeing things, but them what ain't?"

The angel said, "Try asking who took the sticking plaster off Kevin's mouth before he was found."

Debbie thought about it for a minute. "Yeah," she said. "Yeah, I will an' all. That'll fix 'em."

They were passing the bombed site now, no longer picked out in patches of white, but dark and dripping. Only a travesty of the snowman remained — two ghostly

189

mounds, fast disappearing even as they peered through the gate. Debbie remembered the angel saying he would stay until the thaw came and their snowman melted and they didn't need him any more.

"I'm glad you ain't really a baddie," she said. "Can we come all the way home with you and see where you lives?"

"One day," he promised. "But not for a long time yet."

He was standing still now, looking along the road, and at that moment a bus came and stopped at the kerb beside them. Without more ado the angel stepped onto it, smiling and waving goodbye.

They began begging him to stay longer and to come back soon, and trying to find words of thanks all at the same time. Debbie wondered out loud: "What is a angel, anyways?"

The bus was moving away from the pavement.

Marilyn gave her a little push. "Go on, arst him," she said.

"What's a angel?" called Debbie.

"A ANGEL!" shouted Kevin.

"Angel?" echoed the bus conductor. "No, love. You got the wrong number. You wants a thirty or a seventy-three."

The bus was gathering speed now and they could no longer see him distinctly, but his reply came floating clearly back to them on the damp night air.

"A messenger from heaven, my dear children; a bearer of good tidings!"

Then the bus rounded the corner and was gone. They stood looking at each other, alone in the glare of the street lamps.

"Blimey!" said Debbie. "He brung our Kev back,

din't he, Lyn — call that good news?"

They got home to more rejoicing: Terry had returned with a large carrier bag.

"It only just fits the oven!" Mum was saying excitedly. "I got a packet of stuffing and a few sausages . . ."

Cheryl was there too. She wept happily to see the children, but there was a diffidence in her manner which puzzled Debbie under the circumstances. It seemed that when Cheryl had returned to her room she found it occupied by a stranger. Her few belongings had been stacked in the passage outside — except for anything of any value which had disappeared completely. The landlady insisted that as the rent had not been paid and Cheryl had vanished she thought she had gone for good and there was nothing she could do. Both she and the new tenant had locked their doors and refused to discuss the matter further, until eventually Cheryl had taken what she could put in the pram and left. She had wandered along, with no idea where she was going, when a stranger had come up to her — a stout, middle-aged man with a kind smile, who knew her name.

"'E sez he 'ad his tea at the Laughing Cat once," she told Debbie, "but I din't never tell no customer me name. He sez I was to go 'ome, and I sez I bin once, so why go again, and he sez because it's Christmas and you lot's back." Cheryl shrugged. "I can't do nothink else, so I come."

That would explain the atmosphere, thought Debbie. There had clearly been a monumental family row when Cheryl had been there earlier.

"I knew you was here, too," Debbie told her. "I see the pram in the hall. Why'd you leave Karen downstairs?"

Mum dropped the roast tin with a sudden clatter. "You see what?" she demanded.

"I din't think you'd want —" began Cheryl, but Mum interrupted her.

"Sakes alive, child, you can't go leaving the kid by herself down there! She could be 'owling her 'ead off, or baby-snatched or near on anythink these days! Go down and bring her up this instant!"

Cheryl vanished, and in a few minutes reappeared with the familiar puce blanket, its contents protesting at full stretch of her lungs. Mum inspected her critically. Karen's face was spotted and chapped, and there was a yellow stain down the front of her nightdress. Mum put out her arms.

"Give her 'ere," she said sternly.

Cheryl obeyed.

"What'd I tell you?" said Mum. "They don't like being left in strange places. Frightens 'em to death, even at this age." She lifted Karen up onto her shoulder and began to thump her back rhythmically. The yells subsided to a whimper, and the whimper to a series of hiccoughs. Karen began to suck her hand noisily.

"There y'are," said Mum, triumphantly. "They always knows, babies do! She likes her Nan, don't you, duck? There, love, that's better, ain't it? You go to Grandad for a minute, then, while I gets things ready for you."

She dropped Karen into the unsuspecting arms of Dad. He stiffened, and so did Karen, and then a spasm of wind twisted her face into a conspiratorial grin.

"Stone me! See that?" Dad demanded. "Fancy yer old grandad then, do you, sweet'eart? Ain't you just the prettiest little darling?"

And Dad kissed Karen rapturously on the forehead and he and Mum agreed that she was just beautiful.

192

"Oh Dad — Mum —" Cheryl was unable to continue, but no more seemed to be expected of her.

Mum was pulling much-worn baby clothes out of the back of a drawer. "I can 'ave her while yer working, dear," she was saying. "One more don't make that difference. You can 'ave our Lil's room, look."

"'Ere, do us a favour, will you?" said Terry, with mock indignation. "I only bring yer Christmas dinner, din't I? No one don't arst me to stay and have it wiv you. I 'ad me eye on our Gran's room."

But Mum was already pushing chairs together and fetching rugs and blankets. "Don't you worry, son, I'll soon 'ave a bed for you fixed up here, just as often as you wants to come an' lay in it."

Kevin had found a box of things left over from last year's festivities: some crackers, a few streamers, a length of tarnished tinsel and a collapsible plastic Christmas tree. He set this up in the window, draping the tinsel over the branches, while Marilyn fixed a paper star to the top. Debbie offered one end of a cracker to Dad.

"You oughter keep 'em till tomorrow," he said.

"No," said Mum. "Go on, Les. Pull it with 'er now. We'll all pull 'em. We got summink to celebrate tonight, ain't we? We got our kids back — all on 'em!"

She crossed her huge arms, extending two more crackers, her face flushed, her eyes swimming. Dad, a paper streamer sliding over one eyebrow, took hold of another.

"Come on then, everyone," he said. "Take a cracker and all join in a circle, like yer mum and I, look!"

And suddenly Debbie knew what the angel had meant when he said he had come to bring them Christmas: for Cheryl was nursing Karen by the fireside, and

193

Stephen and Carole were curled up asleep together in the big armchair, and Terry had brought them a turkey and was staying to dinner tomorrow, and Marilyn had a pink paper hat on her head and a whole mince pie in her mouth, and Mum and Dad were pulling crackers together, and Kevin was safely back at home again – and Debbie herself had caught a glimpse of Paradise.